A Woman God Can Bless

By

Sharon Norris Elliott

A WOMAN GOD CAN BLESS BY SHARON NORRIS ELLIOTT
Harambee Press is an imprint of LPCBooks
a division of Iron Stream Media
100 Missionary Ridge, Birmingham, AL 35242

ISBN: 978-1-64526-282-4
Copyright © 2020 by Sharon Norris Elliott
Cover design by Hannah Linder
Interior design by AtriTex Technologies P Ltd

Available in print from your local bookstore, online, or from the publisher at: ShopLPC.com

For more information on this book and the author, visit: LifeThatMatters.net

All rights reserved. Noncommercial interests may reproduce portions of this book without the express written permission of LPCBooks, provided the text does not exceed 500 words. When reproducing text from this book, include the following credit line: "*A Woman God Can Bless* by Sharon Norris Elliott published by LPCBooks. Used by permission."

Commercial interests: No part of this publication may be reproduced in any form, stored in a retrieval system, or transmitted in any form by any means—electronic, photocopy, recording, or otherwise—without prior written permission of the publisher, except as provided by the United States of America copyright law.

All Scripture quotations, unless otherwise indicated, are taken from the Holy Bible, New International Version®, NIV®. Copyright ©1973, 1978, 1984, 2011 by Biblica, Inc.TM. Used by permission of Zondervan. All rights reserved worldwide. www.zondervan.com . "NIV" and "New International Version" are trademarks registered in the United States Patent and Trademark Office by Biblica, Inc.TM.

Brought to you by the creative team at LPCBooks: Beatrice Bruno and Edwina Perkins

Library of Congress Cataloging-in-Publication Data
Elliott, Sharon Norris.
A Woman God Can Bless/ Sharon Norris Elliott 1st ed.

Printed in the United States of America

PRAISE FOR
A WOMAN GOD CAN BLESS

A Woman God Can Bless is another example of the delightful teaching gift God has placed in Sharon Norris Elliott. In these pages, you will find clear exposition, practical exercises, and uplifting encouragement to live life as God intends. Every women's group will be challenged, changed, and built up in Christian character as they make this book a vital part of their study.

~Rev. Welton Pleasant II
President of the California State Baptist Convention, vice-president of the Far West Region of the National Baptist Convention, and senior pastor of Christ Second Baptist Church, Long Beach, CA.

We all desire to be blessed by God, and Sharon Elliott walks the reader through how to live out a life God wants to bless. *A Woman God Can Bless* helps the reader think through the promises and practicalities of walking, step by step, with the Almighty, the One and Only who can create the blessed life.

~Pam Farrel,
Author of *7 Simple Skills for Every Woman: Success in Keeping It All Together*

Acknowledgments for *A Woman God Can Bless* by Sharon Norris Elliott

For this and every book I ever write, I am indebted to:

- The Trinity. Thanks to Your book, I have an endless supply of material.
- My Parents. Vincent and Nancy Norris never got a chance to read any of my books because they had moved to Heaven before the first one was published. But what they deposited in me was a love for God and the Church, so my books are my way to keep that legacy alive. Thanks, Momma and Daddy.
- My Husband. James Elliott loves me and believes in me. Thank you, Honey.
- My Children and Grandchildren. Matthew and Mark, your love for your Mom is palpable and helps to keep me alive. We are each other's biggest cheerleaders. Thanks, guys! I love you more than you can say all day! Dallas, Jordyn, and Tahj, you are the cutest and most adorable grandchildren on the planet. Nana loves you! Lori, Jerod, Chad, and your kids – my bonus children, your acceptance makes my life rich.
- Pastor. Pastor Welton Pleasant II. I appreciate your dedication to the Word. Thank you for being a teaching preacher who makes the Bible come alive whenever you teach.

- Every church and conference that has ever invited me to speak. Thank you for believing in my teaching gift.

In addition to acknowledging the people above, I want to acknowledge the special women in my life. So, I send a continual, virtual hug to my ministry mentors and sister-friends, all who have poured into my life, and who live or have lived daily in God's favor as women God can bless.

Ministry Mentors:
Thelma Wells (Mama T), Florence Littauer, Terry Abercrombie, Triette Reeves, Joyce Dinkins.

These women have poured time, prayer, challenges, advice, trust, and love into my life. Their belief in me has moved me forward in ministry and has blessed me more than they will ever know.

Sister-friends:
Michele (Cissi) Watson (BFF), Arneda Mathis, Lanette White, Diana Baxter, and Karynthia Phillips, Tammy Britton – my sisters by other mothers;

Terri Jones, Beverly Turner, Yvonne Norris, Lelar Norris, and Jean Anderson – my sisters-in-law;

Cheryl, Meloni, Nicole, Angela, and Dawn – my nieces;

Teresa Pleasant, my first lady; Rosalind Huggins, my church's LIFT women's ministry leader at Christ Second Baptist Church of Long Beach, CA;

Kathy White, my play daughter; and Tabatha Jones, my daughter-in-law;

Teri Jones, who encouraged me to write my first book;

And,

Jordyn Marie Jones, my grand-daughter who I pray will grow to love and trust in Christ as her Savior, thus becoming (like all these other women who have tremendously blessed my life) a woman God can bless.

Dedication for
A Woman God Can Bless by Sharon Norris Elliott

This book is dedicated to my sister, Saundra Nelson.

Saundra,
I have looked up to you as my super-intelligent sister
Ever since I became the baby in the family
After you had held that spot for 9 years.
You took on your new role as big sister with gusto.

As I've watched your life, I've marveled at how
You always seem to reside in the eye of every storm.

I have watched you cling to God through
disappointments
And surprising life turnabouts,
Handling every change or upheaval
With dignity and grace.

Somehow, you always land on your feet.
I know that your "somehow" is your unshakeable
relationship
With the God we were raised to love and serve.

I dedicate this book to you,
A shining example for all to see
Of a woman God can bless.

Table of Contents

Chapter One: When Theology and Reality Collide..................15

Chapter Two: Put Off..................29

Chapter Three: Put On..................43

Chapter Four: Corrupt Communication versus Speaking Edifying Words: Part One to Husband..................53

Chapter Five: Corrupt Communication versus Speaking Edifying Words: Part Two to Children..................67

Chapter Six: Corrupt Communication versus Speaking Edifying Words: Part Three to Parents, Siblings, and Ex-Husbands..................83

Chapter Seven: Corrupt Communication versus Speaking Edifying Words: Part Four Communicating with Friends and Strangers Gossip, Cursing, Prejudice, Apologetics..................103

Chapter Eight:	Lying versus Speaking the Truth	113
Chapter Nine:	Anger versus Anger without Sin	133
Chapter Ten:	Stealing versus Working	149
Chapter Eleven:	Wrath versus Being Kind	169
Chapter Twelve:	Bitterness versus Being Tenderhearted and Forgiving	183
Chapter Thirteen:	The Renewed, Bless-able You	191

Ephesians 4:17–32

This I say, therefore, and testify in the Lord, that you should no longer walk as the rest of the Gentiles walk, in the futility of their mind, having their understanding darkened, being alienated from the life of God, because of the ignorance that is in them, because of the blindness of their heart; who, being past feeling, have given themselves over to lewdness, to work all uncleanness with greediness.

But you have not so learned Christ, if indeed you have heard Him and have been taught by Him, as the truth is in Jesus: that you put off, concerning your former conduct, the old man which grows corrupt according to the deceitful lusts, and be renewed in the spirit of your mind, and that you put on the new man which was created according to God, in true righteousness and holiness.

Therefore, putting away lying, "Let each one of you speak truth with his neighbor," for we are members of one another. "Be angry, and do not sin": do not let the sun go down on your wrath, nor give place to the devil. Let him who stole steal no longer, but rather let him labor, working with his hands what is good, that he may have something to give him who has need. Let no corrupt word proceed out of your mouth, but what is good for necessary edification, that it may impart grace to the hearers. And do not grieve the Holy Spirit of God, by whom you were sealed for the day of redemption. Let all bitterness, wrath, anger, clamor, and evil speaking be put away from you, with all malice. And be kind to one another, tenderhearted, forgiving one another, even as God in Christ forgave you. (NKJV)

Chapter One

When Theology and Reality Collide

Sometimes the simplest things are the most difficult. Such seems to be the case with actually walking out the beliefs we espouse as Christian women. In many of our cases, I think it is safe to say with few strong contradictions that we believe more than we live. We know that salvation is a free gift we could never deserve. We also know that the acknowledgment of that gift comes with some instructions as to how to best enjoy it.

For example, to enjoy the free gift of salvation to its highest, God says for us to have no other gods before Him. That's a simple instruction, yet we enthrone, or fail to dethrone, our careers, our children, and even the other gifts He has given us, placing Him second, third, or even a distant fourth. God says for us to love our neighbors as we love ourselves. Again, a simple instruction, yet we allow our neighbor to get under our skin and point out their imperfections as an excuse for not extending to them the love God has commanded. God says, "Keep the Sabbath day holy." Simple. Yet here again we complicate the matter with every excuse in the book about why we can't go to church and simply rest and let our bodies replenish.

Indeed, we are masters at complicating what the Master intended to be the simplest things. So, no wonder we can arrive at a place in our lives where we start to wonder whether or not we are women God can bless. Why should God bless us when we have so complicated and convoluted what it means to live as born-again, kingdom women that our claim to be Christians is barely recognizable? Oh, we look great on Sunday morning from 8:00 AM – noon, and we put up a pretty good appearance while working at kids' camp, concentrating at choir rehearsal, and setting up for the upcoming program. However, who are we when we get home? Do we allow the Word of God to penetrate our feelings and comments toward that race of people our parents did not prefer and taught us to mistrust? Do we surrender our thought life to the Word of God when loneliness creeps in and a handsome man's image pops onto the television screen? Do we submit our reactions to the Word of God when our husband says that insensitive thing again?

Here's the thing. We're clear about the surety of our salvation; our place in the kingdom as a daughter of God is secure. The disconnect comes when we read Philippians 2:12b-13 and come face to face with what we are having trouble doing. Each of us is personally charged to "work out your own salvation with fear and trembling; for it is God who works in you both to will and to do for *His* good pleasure" (emphasis mine). This is not a Scripture about obtaining salvation. This is a Scripture about the responsibility we have to now work that salvation out of us. In other words, we must work out the salvation that God has worked in. We must let grow what God has planted; let blossom what He has sown.

As a child, I took eleven years of classical piano lessons. Mrs. Dolly Perry had a little bachelor house in her well-manicured backyard that housed two pianos, several couches, and a small bathroom. Every Thursday for eleven years, my mom drove me to the pink house on the well-manicured street so I could take my lesson. Each week, while sitting at her piano on the right, Mrs. Perry would listen to what I had practiced and then she would teach me a little more by introducing the next skill in the John Thompson series or in *Hanon: The Virtuoso Pianist* book of increasingly more difficult fingering exercises.

Then once a year, at one of the local schools, all of Mrs. Perry's students would gather for the annual recital. Our parents and forced-to-attend siblings would sit through two hours of song after song as we budding musicians nervously yet proudly fingered our way through the pieces we had memorized. We were working out what Mrs. Perry and those books had worked in. If we butchered Bach or mangled Mozart, it was clear to every audience member that we had not spent time in our book practicing. However, if we smoothly sailed through Schubert or Chopin, it was evident we had labored because the rendition was beautifully pleasing to the ear.

God has always intended for us to practice from His book. All the way back in Exodus 24, after God had gotten His people out of their bondage in Egypt,

God communicated His word to the people through Moses. Moses went alone near to God, received God's instructions, and then "came and told the people all the words of the Lord and all the judgments." The people had a unified, admirable reply, the reply all of us should have to God's Word at all times, "All the words which the Lord has said we will do." Afterward, "Moses wrote all the words of the Lord" (Exodus 24:3–4).

As with the children of Israel and as in my piano recital, so it is in our lives as Christian women. God is trying to use His book to instruct us little by little as to how to live as the masterpieces He's created us to be. You do know that "we are His workmanship [His *poema*, His poem, His masterpiece] created in Christ Jesus for good works, which God prepared beforehand that we should walk in them" (Ephesians 2:10, emphasis and explanation added). Our recital for showing off what we have practiced happens every day. Our responsibility is to show—through our actions, words, intentions, deeds, etc.—what He has sown in us. We are on the program to play our piece with our neighbors, colleagues, friends, husbands, children, extended family members, strangers, and society at large.

The point is this: we need to be kingdom women 24/7/365, both when we're on the platform, and also when we don't think anyone is watching. Our challenge is the fact that life hits us with unexpected blows. We become like the Bible's Martha who, four days after the death of her brother, simply couldn't see past her tragedy even though she was looking the Author of life directly in the face. Jesus told her plainly, "Your brother will rise again," and Martha responded a bit sarcastically by reverting to her default knowledge. "I know that he will rise again in the resurrection at the last day." (See John 11:24 NIV.) In other words, Martha was possibly thinking, *Jesus, miss me with the platitudes. Lazarus is dead and You, the one person who could have done something about it, chose to show up too late.*

I can just imagine Jesus taking Martha's tear-stained cheeks in His soon-to-be nail-scarred hands, looking deeply into her eyes and whispering, "I am the resurrection and the life. He who believes in Me, though he may die, he shall live. And whoever lives and believes in Me shall never die. Do you believe this?"

Her answer proved that she obviously was just hurting too much for the great news to register. "Yes, Lord, I believe that You are the Christ, the Son of God, who is to come into the world." (See John 11:23– 27 NKJ.) In other words, again my imagination finds Martha's mind spinning what she refused to say out loud. *Yeah, yeah, yeah. I believe all the stuff You ever said about Yourself, but what good is that to me NOW. I don't need a doctrinal review; I needed Your touch on my dying brother four days ago, and You failed to be here to bless me by touching him. Your theological lessons and my reality just don't match right now.*

We too miss the fact that a theology review is exactly what we always need, especially when we judge that Jesus has failed us. Theology, what is true about God, will always be able to speak to our reality if we put what is true about God above the reality of the situation, rather than the other way around. Our lives are thrown into confusion because we start with our situation and try to force God to fit into it. We are supposed to be so God-aware that we see every circumstance through God-colored lenses. We're to judge all of what we call reality through the everlasting truth of who God is and what God has said.

You see, it's not enough to have God's truth in our brains when it comes to living this Christian life. Unless the truth has infiltrated our hearts, it won't make a hill of beans of a difference when life socks it to us. We may be facing devastating illness, the recent loss of loved ones, heartbreak brought on by children, crippling loneliness— the list of bad stuff happening to good people goes on and on. However, the good news is that God's grace goes on and on too, with mercies that are new every morning! Comfort and deliverance are real despite the circumstances.

With all this talk of grace and new morning mercies, what then could possibly be left to hinder us from receiving blessings? Good question. We could be our own problem. Martha missed her immediate blessing of being comforted because, unlike her sister Mary with whom Jesus shared a good cry, she refused to transfer her hurt into the Master's hands.

In some cases, a lack of blessing may be due to areas of responsibility not yet handled properly on our own part. We can do nothing to obtain salvation or to be plucked out of God's hands, but we do have areas of responsibility to handle properly once salvation is a reality in our lives. Remember once again, we are tasked to "work out [our] own salvation with fear and trembling; for it is God who works in [us] both to will and to do for His good pleasure."

So welcome to this check-up. This book will help us look at our lifestyle, our choices, our habits, and our beliefs, etc., to be sure we are doing our part and are on the right track. Sometimes we get so caught up in the day-to-day vicissitudes of life that we become slipshod in what we would consider to be small details; thus, we place ourselves in a position in which we cannot receive God's blessings.

Now don't misunderstand: God blesses us many times despite us; however, realize that He has put spiritual laws in place that even He follows. For example, the law of sowing and reaping goes far beyond the physical actuality of not seeing a plant grow unless you sow a seed. The spiritual law of sowing and reaping works in the same way; you get what you plant. Peace pervades your atmosphere when you sow calmness. Love surrounds you when you sow kindness. And so on.

Also, don't be embarrassed about having let some things slip. Slipping up happens to all of us. We get into big trouble, though, when we decide to stay down when we fall. Hallelujah that God is a do-over God. He's been allowing do-overs since the beginning.

- The first two kids on earth blew it. Cain killed his brother Abel then got kicked out of the family, so God started a new family line with Seth (Genesis 4:25).
- When God became fed up with all the sin on the planet, He got Noah to help Him avoid having

to create all the animals again, He sent a flood, and He started over (Genesis 6:14– 19).
- God pulled the Israelites out of Egyptian bondage, had them cross the Red Sea on dry land, and then let them witness the Egyptian army drown (Exodus 14:28; 15:21). Then guess what? The Israelites started anew—they got a do-over.

Reality checks and new starts continue through the Bible. For more examples, read the story of the Prodigal Son (Luke 15:11– 32), the water turning to wine (Luke 2:7– 9), and all of the accounts of healings and resurrections.

So, it's clear that God has no problem with giving us reality checks and then chances to get things right. In fact, starting over again is the way to go when stuff is not working. That's how we get a fresh outlook on something with which we're dealing.

My mother, who had been a teenager during America's Great Depression, was a master at keeping it real and then making necessary adjustments. We wore Stride Rite® white leather high-top baby walking shoes. After we had worn them for a while and our feet started growing, Mom would cut the toes out to give our feet more space and her budget more time to save for the next expensive pair. We were the only toddlers on the block with leather, lace-up, peep-toe sandals. (I'm certain that's where I obtained my penchant for beautiful, expensive shoes!) Mom reused foil, plastic bags, and tea bags. At Christmastime, she even found a renewed use for a paper clip. She would unfold it until it looked like an elongated "S". One hooked end would hold an ornament and the other was used to hang the ornament on the tree.

In these and other ways, my mother demonstrated that in life a reality check followed by a do-over from time to time was necessary for refreshment, revival, and extension. In the same way spiritually speaking, we need to check ourselves from time to time to be sure we are living as we should, and then make the appropriate adjustments, so as to receive God's favor and blessings.

Before going on, journal a bit now about the ways in which you initially feel the need for a reality check or a do-over for possible areas in your life that may just be hindering the flow of God's blessings.

1-10-21: Not sure. I am suffering physically more than I ever had in my life, yet I know God has a plan and will use this season for my good and the good of others. I just hope it's not long. I look forward to 2021 and how He wants me to walk with Him.

The Biblical Mandate for Renewal (Prerequisite for Blessing)

Three biblical passages give us our mandate for checking ourselves from time to time to be sure we're on track. First, Paul wrote the book of Romans to a predominantly Gentile audience, and in it sought to explain the basics of the faith. He spent three-fourths of the epistle doing just that. He spent the final fourth of the book, beginning in Romans 12, on the practical outworking of all he had previously taught.

You see, the Roman Christians to whom Paul wrote would have to check themselves out and learn to live their lives an entirely new way. They were used to worshipping many gods and idols and operating on superstition. Now they were being instructed to trust in one God whose teachings were lived out in the life of Jesus Christ, who, by the way, was God incarnate. This was radical and thus it would necessitate a renewal of the mind, a checking out of what old understandings needed to be replaced with new ones.

Vine's Expository Dictionary defines *akainosis*, the Greek word for "renewing" used here, as "the adjustment of the moral and spiritual vision and thinking to the mind of God, which is designed to have a transforming effect upon the life." This is qualitative newness, a renovation which makes a person different from how she was in the past.

We went through a change something like this when we reached adolescence, minus the "mind of God" part. As little girls, most of us waited impatiently for our breasts to bloom. Then when they did, whether their size was our pride or our anguish, along came something else upon which we had not bargained—the incomparable menstrual cycle. And hasn't that been the bane of our existence ever since?

Our bodies and our psyches went through a qualitative change, a renewal that made us a different person from who we had been in the past. Our new sense of womanhood may have made us more interested in makeup, nails, and our hair. Hopefully, our mothers taught a new level of discretion. Our clothes and shoes really mattered, too. I remember graduating from tights to nylons, flats to heels, and, of course, T-shirts to bras. And those BOYS! How the boys began to recognize us and we certainly began to recognize them. We loved checking out this new reality. Ah, the renewal!

But I digress. You get the idea.

Second, Paul relays the same basic message in his letter to the Ephesians when he writes in verse 23:

> …and be renewed in the spirit of your mind

Vine's Expository Dictionary again explains the Greek word used here for "renewed." *Ananeoo* means renovate and reform. This renewal "under the controlling power of the indwelling Holy Spirit, directs its bent and energies Godward" to enjoy fellowship with God and Jesus Christ, and to fulfill God's will. This definition adds to the Romans passage. Not only are we to behave differently from how we did in the past, but we are to do so with new spiritual vitality. This would be like not only moving into adolescence, but finally feeling okay with the changes.

Finally, in Colossians 3:10, Paul tells his readers the following:

> …and have put on the new man who is renewed in knowledge according to the image of Him who created him…

Here we come to understand that the renewal includes another checkpoint or measuring rod, a complete and true knowledge of what Christ would have us to be.

So, the three stages of a good reality check and a total renewal are as follows: First, a radical change initiated by God begins to take place, like the onset of adolescence. Then after a while, we become comfortable in our new "skin" and we begin to allow the Holy Spirit to direct us. Finally, we start really understanding our new state, like emerging fully into womanhood.

R.I.S.E.

Radical change.

Initiated by God.

Submission to the Holy Spirit's direction.

Emergence into full understanding (and readiness to pass the information on).

This book will take us through a process through which we will R.I.S.E. This process will hopefully lead to renewal and thus place us into position to better represent the kingdom of God. The study of this one passage—Ephesians 4:17-32—by no means covers all the areas in our lives that need checking out, but it is a good, practical place to start. Once we move into the core of the study, you may at first think these to be trivial matters, but I urge you to probe your heart. You'll see, as I did, that renovation in these areas is crucial to the well-being of your Christian walk and growth, and to moving into the position of being a woman whom God can bless.

Chapter Two

Put Off

Some of you may remember typing school papers on a typewriter. If you are young enough to have always had a screen rather than a piece of paper to type your words upon, let me tell you what creating a research paper was like.

After leaving the comforts of home, you would spend hours in the library searching through the card catalog (long, thin drawers of index cards that had been individually typed with relevant information about each and every book in the building) for books related to your topic. You'd write down titles of the books and the numbers of the Dewey Decimal System that would be found on the spines, then begin the mad search through the library to pull those books from the shelves. Once all the books were gathered, you would search through the Periodical Indexes to find up-to-date articles about your subject. Since no one was allowed to check magazines and newspapers out of the library, you would have to use the copy machine and spend a small fortune (at a cost of five to ten cents per copy) to take the pages of the articles home with you to read.

With all those books checked out and all the copies of the articles packed up, you would trudge home. Soon, those books and articles would be spread all over your bed as you read through them, writing notes from each on lined paper. Finally, you would be able to stack the books on one side of your desk and start to combine your notes into the sections of your paper. Once those sections were written out in longhand (that means you would actually write every sentence on pages and pages of a yellow legal pad of paper), then you would sit at the typewriter and type out what you had written.

Then came the frustrating part: fitting the paragraphs on the pages when footnotes had to also fit on the page. And please do not make a mistake. Mistakes meant one of three things: typing the whole page again, erasing the incorrectly typed letters (if you had been smart enough to use erasable onion skin typing paper), or painting Wite-Out over the mistake. No one wanted to keep starting over, and erasable paper was more expensive than regular paper, so most people usually chose the white-out option and worked extremely hard at not making mistakes.

One more complication existed: teachers did not like it if too much Wite-Out was used on any one page, so you would have to be sure the liquid was thin enough to dry quickly and almost disappear, but thick enough to actually cover the mistake. In an effort to both cover your mistakes but also please your teachers, the wrong letters you had typed would sometimes poke through under the correct letters. And you'd inevitably lose points for the polka-dot pages with mistakes showing through under the alterations.

Well, thankfully the above frustrations in typing papers no longer exist, but the same problems persist when it comes to dealing with things on a spiritual level. We put in lots of work to cover up, adjust, and camouflage our old ways rather than simply putting them off (throwing them away) and starting over, as we should have done by retyping our papers. Old ways of thought and behavior cannot just be painted over; they must first be identified, then completely discarded. Just like we cannot turn in a research report spot-colored with Liquid Paper and then typed over with other letters, so it is that we cannot superimpose God's directions for living over our old ways of doing things.

Ephesians 4:22 explicitly teaches what we are to do.

Read the following passages and paraphrase their meanings:

2 Timothy 2:21 _Those who can themselves can be instruments for God's Holy Good work_

Psalms 119:9 _Stay on path of purity by living according to God's Word._

2 Corinthians 7:1 _Purify self from anything that contaminates the body + spirit to be holy + reverent for God._

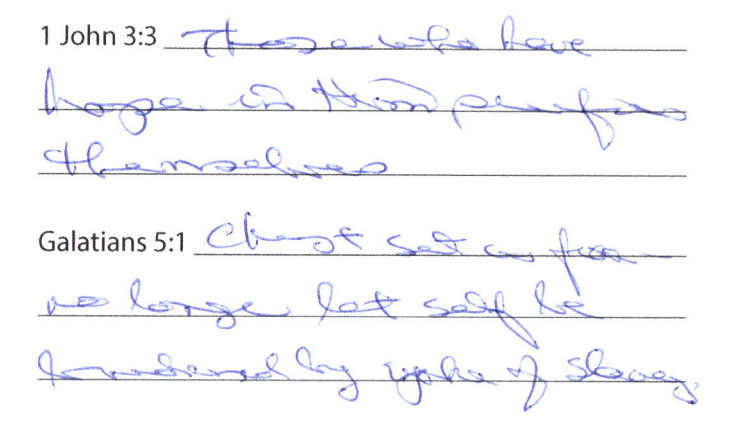

1 John 3:3 _Those who have hope in Him purifies themselves_

Galatians 5:1 _Christ set us free, no longer let self be burdened by yoke of slavery_

Check yourself: What attitudes, actions, judgments, or justifiers are you wearing under the exquisite outer garment of your spirituality? Let's go straight to the heart of the matter. If we intend to be women God can bless, we need to ask ourselves some pertinent questions:

- Are we really who we say we are?
- Are we on a continual journey to set aside all that is not like Christ, replacing whatever we set aside with Christlikeness?
- ==More important than walking and talking like He does: do we think like He does?==
- In every situation— even in the mundane, everyday-ness of life— are we coming from the same place He's coming from?
- Are we both "in" this world and "of" it too, so much like our present post-modern culture in thought, word, and deed that no one can tell the difference between us and an unsaved person if they didn't know us personally?

When we are excited about our new life in Christ, it can sometimes actually seem easy to "put off" some things in favor of the wonder of our newfound love of the Savior. We gladly stop going certain places, watching certain TV shows, listening to certain types of music, and may even clean up our language a little. However, some of the not-so-obvious quirks can be left unchecked, the well-entrenched addictions are not kicked, and the illicit relationships are not immediately "put off." After all, we're comfortable with our painted-over mistakes." They have come to define us and we are not quite sure of what we would be without them.

God expects us to operate as totally new creatures in Christ, and it is upon these "new creatures" that He bestows His choicest blessings. What seems right to us isn't necessarily right to Him. We cannot allow ourselves to be lulled into believing false realities. True reality comes as we think like Christ and adopt His ways. What the world believes is right is the false reality. How are we, then, to start to live according to God's reality rather than the world's? I'm glad you asked. Let's start by exploring this "put off" instruction.

Who Is Responsible?

Who is responsible for doing the "putting off" or changing? That's easy; we are. The verse above says that we are to do the work of putting off or turning from the way we used to do things. Notice that even though God will be there to help us, He is not going to do this for us, nor will our ungodly habits simply fall off on their own.

Every habit, positive or negative, has been developed, or has to be developed in our lives as a result of practice. For example, regularly checking my rear-view mirror as I drive is a habit I have developed and have kept up for over forty-five years. This good driving habit has helped keep me safe on the road; however, I haven't always checked the rear-view in relation to my decisions about men.

I habitually used to choose men to date who needed more help from me than they could provide for me. Until I realized my poor choices were a result of a habit I had developed, I kept practicing or exercising those choices. Until I put off that habit of choosing needy men, I was not able to incorporate the types of relationship choices God would have me make. It was totally my responsibility to put off choosing men my way. Once I put that bad habit off, I could put on the habit of listening to God's guidance and incorporating God's methods concerning how to choose whom I would date. Once I had put off my ways and put on His ways, I found myself in position to receive God's blessing on my relationships, which culminated in meeting my wonderful husband. It was totally my responsibility to put off whatever my former lifestyle choices had taught me to do and think about male/female dating relationships.

A great biblical example of someone who exercised his positive habits and was blessed by God as a result is Daniel. From the time he was stolen away from his homeland by the conquering Chaldeans led by King Nebuchadnezzar, he "purposed in his heart that he would not defile himself" with that which the king gave him and his friends to eat. Daniel's determination paid off. By unwaveringly sticking to exactly what his faith had taught him to do, the results God intended came about. When he and his friends were tested and compared with the other young men who had accepted the king's diet, Daniel and his buddies were ten times better in every area. King Nebuchadnezzar ended up promoting them. (See Daniel chapter 1.)

Then Daniel continued to work faithfully for this heathen king and found himself in another situation in which he could let the power of his God shine. The king had a troubling dream and demanded that his magicians, astrologers, and wise men tell him both the dream and the interpretation, or he would kill them and their households. Daniel and his friends would have been among those killed. Instead, they prayed, and God revealed the dream and interpretation to him. He told the king but ascribed the interpretation to God. Not only did Daniel save his own life and spare the lives of those others who had been marked for death, but he witnessed to the power of God, getting Nebuchadnezzar to fall "on his face, prostrate before Daniel." The king also said, "Truly your God is the God of gods, the Lord of kings, and a revealer of secrets, since you could reveal this secret." Then the king promoted Daniel and gave him many great gifts; and he made him ruler over the whole province of Babylon, and chief administrator over all the wise men of Babylon" (See Daniel chapter 2).

Daniel was responsible for doing what he had been taught that God wanted him to do. He simply decided to obey God's dietary laws as a way to continue to honor his God although he was living in a culture that did not honor his God. Daniel had no idea that eating vegetables and drinking water would lead him into a high governmental position. And he wasn't obeying God in order to get something special from Him. Daniel was obeying God because it was right to obey God. Period. The blessing was in God's mind, not in Daniel's, but the blessing became a reality for Daniel due to Daniel's obedience in the little things.

What are some of your positive habits?

Timely, organized

How did you develop the above habits?

From parents or natural tendency.

How can you use some of the above techniques to develop good spiritual habits?

Same.

Name some small way you obey God without really even thinking about it.

_____

_____

_____

Why Must the Former Lifestyle Go?

Why should we put off our former lifestyle? Again, Ephesians 4:22 gives the answer, saying the old man's former way of life is "being corrupted by its deceitful desires." Something that is being corrupted is being made rotten, sick, and no longer any good.

We can compare our former lifestyle or way of thinking to a corrupted computer disk or flash drive. Many of us may now trust the cloud (wherever that is) in which to store our electronic files, but I am still backing things up by saving files and photos on flash drives and on my computer's hard drive. After I have saved my information on a flash drive, I can go back to that drive, pull up what I have stored, and use that information again. But at times, although at one point the computer could read the information the drive contained, something devastating can go wrong. Perhaps a virus was introduced or the drive was exposed to something external that messed it up. Whatever the case, the computer can no longer read the information stored there, so the flash drive is no good; it's corrupted. Our only option is to throw it away, get a new flash drive, and start again. Hopefully, if we're wise, we will not expose the new disk to the same destructive forces that spoiled the old one. And we would never even consider trying to put new information on that bad drive.

Our old lifestyle is like that corrupted flash drive. Our salvation has upgraded us. There's information on the old drive that our born-again computer cannot read. The internal virus of the sin nature and the external exposure to humanistic thoughts have corrupted and continue to corrupt our old "drive." All it is now good for is to be thrown away. It's time for a new flash drive to be plugged in, and new information from the Holy Spirit to be uploaded into our lives.

Now you may be thinking, "My lifestyle's not that messed up. I just need a little tuning up in some areas."

Ladies, reality check. I know it's hard to face up to the rotten side of ourselves, but that's a central purpose of this book. Think about this. We've all seen a woman walking down the street or in the mall wearing a horrendous outfit that is fighting to cover the body that's bursting through it. We shook our heads as we drove or walked past, thinking, *Didn't she look in the mirror before she left home?* Well, if we refuse to look at our messed-up habits, we are just like that sister we're criticizing. Believe this: Others see that the Christianity we profess is struggling to cover the raunchy character that will inevitably burst through.

Ask yourself these questions:

In what ways does my profession of Christianity make me different from my secular friends and acquaintances?

Lifestyle, how I talk, dress, hang with, where I go/don't go

Is there a visible difference between my lifestyle and that of people I know who have no relationship with God?

Yes.

How Did My Former Lifestyle Get So Bad?

So again, with God's help, it is our personal responsibility to put off our former lifestyle, and we must put that lifestyle off because it is corrupt. The question arises, how did the old me get corrupt in the first place? Good question. Ephesians 4:22 answers this one, too. The old me is corrupted thanks to "deceitful lusts." What are those, you ask? Deceitful lusts are our forbidden longings and desires that deceive or delude us. In other words, the old me is corrupted because I brought the corruption on myself.

I hear your thoughts again. *Come on, Sharon. You're going too far. You want me to believe that I have corrupted myself?* Yes, that's exactly what I'm saying; however, you know I wouldn't be saying this without back-up, so look at Ephesians 4:17-19:

> *So I tell you this, and insist on it in the Lord, that you must no longer live as the Gentiles do, in the futility of their thinking. They are darkened in their understanding and separated from the life of God because of the ignorance that is in them due to the hardening of their hearts. Having lost all sensitivity, they have given themselves over to sensuality so as to indulge in every kind of impurity, and they are full of greed.*

Paul tells us not to walk (live) like we used to walk (live). And how was that? We used to behave like other Gentiles—people who did not know the Lord. They live in the vanity of their minds, basically doing whatever they deem best. They greedily do wrong because, being alienated from God, they just don't know any better.

Even if we grew up as "the good girl," we're not off the hook. The Bible states, "There is no one righteous, not even one; there is no one who understands, no one who seeks God" (Romans 3:10-11 NIV). Without a total surrender to Christ, by default we're guilty before Him. Insidious sins, which can sometimes be difficult to see, abide within us. Pride, jealousy, bitterness, and unforgiveness—just to name a few—could very well be lurking under that goody-goody façade.

The old me or the old you does whatever it wants because it doesn't know any better. We may even label our decisions "common sense," not realizing that unless this common sense is based upon God's Word, it's still corrupted sense. The old me and the old you are alienated from God through ignorance and blindness. And our continued sinful behavior and thought life cause continual corruption.

A woman once poured her heart out to me, wondering why she was single and seemingly unable to find a good man. As she talked, I realized that she was intelligent and articulate. I did notice, however, her unkempt appearance. She wore an oversized, stretched-out T-shirt, unstructured loose pants, and shoes with worn-over heels. Her hair had been hastily (and not very neatly) pulled into a ponytail. As we talked, I slid some of my philosophy into the conversation. I shared how, when I was single, I realized that if I were to get married, I'd meet my husband one day. Since I didn't know when that day would be, I left my house each day pulled together, just in case that day would be the day we'd cross paths. Without missing a beat, and seemingly uninspired by my little story, she told me she liked to feel comfortable and was waiting to meet a man who could love her as is.

This sister did not even realize she practiced a habit that contributed to the very dilemma about which she was complaining. I doubt seriously that she would be attracted to any man who practiced her same dressing habits.

We are so used to the way we've always done things and how we've always thought, we don't even realize that it very well could be our own way of thinking that is keeping us down. When we refuse to acknowledge the truth of God, God gives us over to what we want to believe and our own lusts destroy us. We insist on having for ourselves what God does not want for us. We insist on believing a false reality. In other words, we actually insist upon doing that which God simply will not bless.

So, ladies, now that you realize you are walking around with corrupt thoughts and habits that you helped bring upon yourself, face up to the challenge to take the responsibility for putting off that old lifestyle.

Chapter Three

Put On

Jesus taught His disciples that when an unclean spirit leaves a person, the spirit roams around seeking another dwelling. When it can't find one, it returns to its original host. When the spirit finds that dwelling all cleaned out but empty, it returns, bringing multiple, more evil spirits along. This new condition leaves the person—the original dwelling—in a much worse state than he suffered at first (See Matthew 12:43– 45).

I relate that truth to you because I know you are convinced from the last chapter of your need to put off your former lifestyle. But before we get down to the nuts and bolts of enumerating the thoughts, actions, and habits that must go, I want to also convince you to replace them with the thoughts, actions, and habits God suggests. The balance of putting off our former lifestyle is found in Ephesians 4:24:

> …and to put on the new self, created to be like God in true righteousness and holiness.

As with the instruction to put off the old man, the putting on of the new man is our responsibility too. Godly habits and reactions are not just going to start happening. It is vital that we deliberately fill the spaces left empty as we kick the old habits out.

Mary, one of my girlfriends, gave up smoking some years ago. She was convinced of the health benefits, but she had not realized that the habit extended outward beyond her lungs. Along with smoking came habits associated with how she was using her hands and having something in her mouth. For example, after meals she'd reach for a cigarette and spend the next ten minutes or so with her hands and mouth involved in the smoking activity. When she quit, her lungs were grateful, but her hands and mouth were at a loss as to what to do with themselves. She unconsciously reached for candy, chips—anything available to keep her hands and mouth busy. She didn't even recognize the connection until her roommate—and the extra pounds she was gaining—made it obvious.

Both physically and spiritually, the principle is the same. When we give up a habit, a vacuum is created. Something *will* fill the void. If we aren't vigilant, that filler will be something negative. It takes deliberately practicing a positive new habit in order for it to become the void-filler.

Will You Want This New Lifestyle?

Change can be traumatic. Although we are sold on the fact that some of our old habits have to go, we may not be sold on the fact that change will actually be better for us. Many times we keep doing the same stuff, even if it's destructive, because we are simply used to doing it that way. It's not certain that Albert Einstein said it, but if he did, he spoke a truth about this habit when he said, "A sure sign of insanity is doing the same thing over and over and expecting a different result." Child abusers and alcoholics never intended to become what they've turned out to be. In many cases, they are just imitating what they grew up seeing in their parents. They hated the offending parent or parents and vowed never to become like them. Then, when they grew up and the challenges of life arose, they retreated to the only coping mechanism they knew, abuse or alcohol use. And the cycle continued.

I told you earlier in this book about how I had a habit of choosing the wrong kind of man. I kept breaking up with the guys, cleaning them out of my life, but not refilling the space with better choice options. Consequently, I would allow the same species of wolf to infiltrate my heart. I needed to totally redefine my taste. This is what you'll have to do too with any lifestyle change you are trying to make.

Are there any negative habits you can now identify that you find yourself constantly repeating? List them here:

_____

_____

_____

_____

Now find Scriptures that substantiate the fact that these are negative habits:

_____

_____

_____

_____

Now find other Scriptures that give you positive replacement habits:

_____

_____

_____

_____

(For the above activity, you may want the help of your pastor or a close, mature Christian friend.)

Second Corinthians 5:17 (KJV) says, "Therefore if any man be in Christ, he is a new creature: old things are passed away; behold, all things are become new." Becoming new is a process. It's what the putting off and putting on is all about. This process reminds me of when I was planning my wedding and I went to the bridal boutique to choose my dress.

In order to fit into my bridal gown, I first had to take off all my other clothes. I even had to purchase a new and different type of undergarment in order for my beautiful new dress to fit properly.

You see, my wedding gown represented the start of my new life. Not only did I have to shed the old in order to fit into the new, I had to be sure I had just the right dress. I could not just wear any old dress, it had to be special. The popular television show, *Say Yes to the Dress* had not launched, so I was on my own finding my dream dress. I had combed through bridal magazines and chosen a form-fitting, mermaid style, beaded lace gown. However, when I got to the boutique and tried it on, that style looked horrible on me. Then I tried on a few other choices with the same result. Finally, I turned to the expert personal designer the store had assigned to me. She had been listening to my desires for a romantic, elegant look and had been studying my body type.

"I think I have the perfect dress for you," she said.

Realizing my choices had failed miserably, I relented. She helped me into the gown she had selected and when I emerged from the dressing room and turned to the mirror, I could hardly believe it was my own reflection looking back. The simple A-line satin strapless gown with the dropped waist hugged my figure. The understated beading and crystal trim along the top were just enough to communicate the grace and sophistication I wished to convey.

We can trust what God chooses for us in the same way I could trust that designer. I gave up my right to my choice for my gown when I realized the designer had more experience at matching gowns with brides. Guess what? God has more experience matching habits with success, and we can comfortably give up our right to our choices in life for ourselves in deference to His. You will want the lifestyle God has chosen for you because He knows you, your desires, and your style better than you do. He knows what will fit best.

Why Will a New Lifestyle Work?

The new lifestyle will work because it is created by God. It is created after or modeled after God. (See Ephesians 4:24 again.) We know from Genesis chapter one that everything God creates is good. Let's also look at 2 Corinthians 3:18:

> And we all, who with unveiled faces contemplate the Lord's glory, are being transformed into his image with ever-increasing glory, which comes from the Lord, who is the Spirit.

The more we look at Christ, spending time with Him beholding His glory, the more like Him we will be. It follows then if we become more like the Lord, whose life definitely worked like it was supposed to, our lives will work like they're supposed to work also.

Isn't it funny how friends who spend lots of time together begin to exhibit the same habits, use the same phraseology, and respond with the same logic? Couples who have been married many years even start to look alike. That's because association breeds assimilation. This psychological principle is also the basis of peer pressure. Even a cursory glance at a group of teenage girls together in a mall is proof of the truth of this principle.

So, as we hang around Christ and His Word, we'll see that His habits will work wondrously as replacements for our old ones and will make us more like Him.

How Is the New Lifestyle Able to Work?

Whenever I'm cooking hamburgers, I never use my toaster. Imagine that. It's a perfectly good toaster. It heats up and it even has a control that allows me to decide how long I want it to cook my food. Still, I never use it to cook hamburgers. It's pretty obvious why. My toaster was not designed to cook meat. As a matter of fact, if I did put hamburger meat in it, I would ruin both the meat and the machine.

We have been operating with some of our habits like putting meat in a toaster. The stuff we're doing is stuff we were never meant to do, and that's why our lifestyle isn't working to bring God's blessings our way. When we begin to operate in accordance with the lifestyle God intends, we'll be amazed at how quickly we'll see a difference.

Denise* had been in church most of her life, but she was only nominally obedient to the mandates of the Word of God. She was going through life making her own choices, some of which were directly opposed to God's commandments. She had several children out of wedlock and was basically careening through life one trauma after another.

Denise then decided to live life God's way, starting by making His habits her own. Since that decision, she has given multiple praise reports, the latest being the news of receiving a brand-new car just one week after a car accident destroyed her old one yet left her with no injuries.

Am I promising you that none of life's afflictions will assail you once you dig in your heels and decide to do things God's way? Unfortunately, no, I cannot promise you that. However, what I can promise is that you will now have a heavenly companion traveling with you as you pass down whatever road becomes your next route. We can be encouraged to know that our new habits will work to effectively fill the void left by the ousting of the old ones, because we will start living the way we were created to live. We will be living like Christ and will be following His lead. We will be operating in cooperation with our God-given design.

Look at Ephesians 2:10:

> For we are God's handiwork, created in Christ Jesus to do good works, which God prepared in advance for us to do.

The word "workmanship" is from the Greek word *poiema*, which literally means "product." We are literally God's poem. He has created us—composed us as He would a poem—for good works and He has ordained that we should walk in those good works throughout our lives. In order to walk in those good works, and thereby receive God's favor as women God can bless, we will have to put off the old man and put on the new one.

The rest of this book will deal with the specifics of what should be put off and what should be put on. I'd like to suggest that we RISE. For the rest of this book, we will use this acronym to help us become women God can bless.

R.I.S.E.

Radical change. What is out of whack in my habits, thoughts, or actions that need to be radically changed?

Initiated by God. What is Scripture telling me about this/these issue(s)?

Submission to the Holy Spirit's direction. How is the Holy Spirit directing me to carry out the necessary changes?

Emergence into full understanding (and readiness to pass the information on). Upon making the necessary lifestyle changes, in what ways am I being led to share my new understanding with those around me?

Chapter Four

Corrupt Communication versus Speaking Edifying Words: Part One To Husband

Let no corrupt word proceed out of your mouth, but what is good for necessary edification, that it may impart grace to the hearers. Ephesians 4:29 (NKJV)

Ephesians chapter four contains the list of habits associated with our old lifestyle that must be put off. We're going to start right off the bat dealing with that which gets many of us into more trouble than anything else— our mouths. So, our first focus will concentrate on the habit of the old man the Bible calls "corrupt communication."

Definition

We have already discussed the meaning of the word "corrupt." Here, as an adjective describing communication, it still means rotten and worthless. Communication carries the meaning of "intelligible speech," so corrupt communication can be understood to be rotten, worthless words that come out of our mouths that someone else understands to be directed at him or her. We are talking about unwholesome talk that does not build others up.

The flip side of corrupt communication is speech that edifies or builds others up—words that come out of our mouths that someone else understands and appreciates as useful, helpful, and encouraging.

Remember, when we put off the habit of corrupt communication, there will be a vacuum created that will hunger to be filled. We will still engage in conversations and confrontations and will usually want to have something to say. For example, we may have been raised in a home where children were seen and not heard. We vowed that when we grew up, we were always going to speak our minds. Then we began to come into adulthood through the women's liberation movement, and now that we're grown, we do just that. However, our comments may sometimes be caustic and hurtful.

"But it's the truth," you say, "and the truth is the light. I'm just setting people straight."

Granted, we may be telling the truth. The problem is not what we're saying but how and why we're saying it. Every truth doesn't necessarily have to be broadcast at that time, in that manner, or at all. ==If our truth does not build up the hearers, it qualifies as corrupt communication.==

Our challenge then is to replace unwholesome speech with words that build. More easily said than done, you say? Okay, you know I'm not going to leave you hanging out there with no practical help.

Let's deal directly with three specific types of corrupt communication: put-downs, cursing, and gossip. We'll look at some examples of how we may be pulling people apart with each and discuss some positive replacement building words.

Put-Downs

The most direct form of unwholesome talk is an outright put-down. Our tongues can be good at cooperating with our negative emotions and uttering words that hurt others. James chapter 3 says that our tongues are the most difficult part of our whole body to tame and we hurt other people with it.

My friend Lily* used to get herself into lots of scraps whenever her mouth ran ahead of her brain. She was quick to utter accurate yet distasteful, sarcastic remarks. After such comments, she would turn to me and question, "Did I say that out loud?" The answer was usually yes and we'd have to make excuses or beat a hasty retreat to avoid either further embarrassment or an unfavorable confrontation.

Lily, you, and I, and every woman who wants to be blessed by God, simply must gain control of our tongues in this area. There are several ways as women that we engage in the corrupt communication of put-downs.

Put-Downs Toward our Husbands

From the time we are very little girls, many of us dreamed of being married. We fantasized about settings from a small, intimate chapel in the country to a candlelit cathedral with a long, center, flower-strewn aisle for a grand processional. Some of us pictured an outdoor garden ceremony while others saw ourselves uniting on a tropical beach at sunset. Gown styles, number of attendants, type of reception, ring designs— all of these details differed according to our individual dreams, as our wedding fantasy swam around in our heads.

What didn't vary much was our bottom-line requirement for the husband. We wanted a man who would love us and make us feel special. When those of us who are married think back to the early days of our love affair with our husbands, many of us can remember how our hearts fluttered and our cheeks blushed as we caught ourselves smiling just thinking about him. After all, we'd found Mr. Right. (For example, from early on in my relationship with my husband, he would wink at me. His winks and sexy smiles still give me goose bumps and butterflies.)

How do we get from our dreams of the perfect wedding and the perfect man to uttering corrupt communication about him and the life we have with him? Maybe we're disillusioned by reality. He wakes up with bad breath, crust in the corners of his eyes, and disheveled hair. Then he disappears behind the morning paper when we're ready to rattle off our plans for the day. Perhaps it has taken longer than expected to reach a certain planned level of success. It could be that we paid more attention to planning the wedding than we did to planning the marriage. Or maybe we just flat out made a poor choice.

Whatever the case, we are engaging in corrupt communication if we're speaking to our husbands disrespectfully. Ephesians 5:33 (NKJV) ends by commanding wives to reverence their husbands.

> …and let the wife see that she respects her husband.

I know what you're thinking. *"Command" is such a harsh word.*

Sorry, ladies, but when the Bible tells you to do something, let something happen, and see to it that something takes place; those are commands. The above passage says, "… and the wife see that …" This means for you to see to it, be sure you take care of this.

My friend Karen is allergic to milk products. She has learned to "see to it" that nothing she is ever served has been prepared with them. She is sure to take care of this because if she doesn't, the physical consequences are devastating.

It's the same with my friend Teresa. She can eat shellfish, but she is acutely allergic to any other kind of fish. Once my husband and I were out to dinner with her and her husband. My husband and I ordered steaks, her husband ordered a fish dish, and she ordered lamb chops. After we had all been served and had started eating, her husband reached his fork over to her plate to point at which lamb chop he wanted to try. Startled, she asked him, "Did you just touch that with your fork? You did that on purpose. Just take the whole thing." Her allergy would not allow her to eat something that even his fork had touched if his fork had previously been touching that fish. She was "seeing to it" that she did not come in contact with that which could cause her the discomfort of a bad allergic reaction.

We see to things that we deem important. We see to it that our children are properly fed, housed, clothed, and kept healthy. We see to it that we get our paychecks. We see to it that we care for our own bodies. We should have the same attitude about seeing to it that we reverence our husbands in every way, but in our current discussion, we're concentrating on reverencing them with our words.

I hear you thinking again. *But "reverence" is going way overboard.*

Now you're arguing with Scripture itself because that's the word used. Hold on though, it gets even more dramatic. The Greek word translated 'reverence' is *phobeo*, from which we get our English word phobia or fear. So reverencing your husband means you deal with him—and that includes speaking to him--as you would a person you look up to or for whom you have profound respect.

I once felt compelled to share with my boss a fault of his that was affecting our entire workplace. I did not enter this conversation carelessly. Attempting to lighten the mood from the start, I asked, "How much can I say without getting fired?" He was amused and very open, I did not share my thoughts and feelings about him in an accusatory tone, and the outcome of the conversation was positive.

If I take that much care when talking to my boss at work, I should see to it that I speak with my husband in at least the same, if not with an even more respectful tone and attitude. Doing so is a sign of giving my husband the reverence God has told me to see to.

"But Sharon, you don't know my husband. He doesn't know how to act."

I don't need to know your husband to know that the Scripture still applies to you. You're told to reverence him, period. The verse says nothing about how "reverencible" he acts. We owe our obedience to God's Word, not to our circumstances.

My husband is very opinionated and he's strong about the way he expresses those opinions. When we enter into discussions on topics about which we disagree, it frustrates me to communicate with him because he talks over me. He talks louder and talks more and sometimes I feel as though he is not considering the merits of my side of the issue. Raising my voice doesn't help. Not only am I not verbally combative in that way, but I really do care about whatever we're discussing, and I desire to be understood. Besides, I know I'm commanded to speak to him respectfully, and I also know the Bible confirms that "a gentle answer turns away wrath, but a harsh word stirs up anger" (Proverbs 15:1, NIV).

I have learned to listen and pose some questions so that I'm totally clear on his point. Instead of giving in to the intimidation I feel, I quietly yet firmly state my case. Sometimes I have to remind him to listen to me as I've listened to him. I've also learned to back up my opinions with facts I find in books or on the internet. Google, here I come!

There are also times when I judge that the conversation just will not have a resolution. It's in those times that I simply stop talking. I don't roll my eyes, sigh loudly, nor concede my point. I just stop talking. As an intelligent man, he realizes that it's useless to argue with the air. This is usually a very frustrating position to have to take, but I simply refuse to disrespect him with my words. At times, the discussion may come up again on another day when the emotion of the present moment has passed. At other times, that particular issue just dissolves on its own and we forget about it. Both my husband and I are strong on our views, but I've discovered that once he allows a new viewpoint to ruminate—even if that rumination takes a while—occasionally he will reconsider his position.

My husband would not even consider my ideas if I insisted upon presenting them to him disrespectfully. He would be so focused on my rude behavior that my words would evaporate. It's worth sucking it up and taking the extra effort to honor him in order to both make my point and build our marriage.

Check Yourself

How do you speak to your husband? Do you speak to him reverently and respectfully or irreverently and disrespectfully? Conduct a survey. Ask the above two questions of yourself, your children, your husband, and any others who frequently watch you interact with your husband.

Corrupt Communication versus Speaking Edifying Words

My answer: _A little of both._

My children's answer:

_____

Others' answers: _____

_____

My husband's answer: _____

_____

If the above answers reveal that you are not honoring your husband with your speech, deliberately change the way you respond to him. Determine to put off your disrespectful tone. When you feel yourself becoming caustic, stop talking. Take a moment to think through what you want to say. The most important thing is your obedience to God in relation to how you speak to your husband. Next, focus on what really needs to be expressed. Then if necessary, calmly, rationally, and respectfully make your point and then shut up. You don't have to agree that moment, the next day, or ever, but you do have to reverence your husband every day.

Think of some creative ways to show your husband how much you reverence him. As a writer, my most effective means of communication is through notes. Every now and then, I leave my husband a note to tell him how much I appreciate who he is to me. My husband worked for the power company, so I once put a sticky note on his steering wheel that said, "I'm thankful for how you keep yourself safe at work." I knew he appreciated that when, visiting his office one day, I noticed he had that note posted above his desk. Start a list here of some ways you can communicate your reverence to your husband.

___

___

___

___

Another way you use corrupt communication in connection with your husband is when you talk negatively about him to others. I'm not including talks you may need to have with your pastor, a counselor, or a mentor when there's some serious trouble. As Jada Pinkett Smith, a Hollywood actress with a strong marriage, asserts, "Everybody needs a Sister Souljah in their life. She's one of the most intelligent women I know...and she's a great mediator. If you have somebody in your life who can do that, it's very helpful " (*Ebony*, September 2004).

However, when you dump your frustrations about your husband on others because you want some sympathy, you could create a problem. When you do this, you degrade him in their eyes. Even when you and your husband get past your argument, those with whom you shared will likely still feel negatively toward him.

The media is good at filling us in on the foibles and failures of celebrities. What do we most remember? We can readily recall the divorces, affairs, public arguments, and social blunders we hear about repeatedly on television and in the papers. The next time that star comes out in a movie, our conversation about him or her will turn to the latest negative report we heard.

If this happens in our memories for people we don't even know personally, how much more will it be true that the negative comments about your husband will take root in your friends' minds? Work on replacing the habit of sharing your husband's faults with a new habit of patience to work things out with him.

Before you start the activities below, remember that all things relating to our Christian lives should be done in balance. God forbid that you are in an abusive relationship. If you are, it is imperative that you get yourself to safety. You do not deserve to be physically and emotionally harmed. You are not to blame for bringing harsh treatment upon yourself. There are safe places for you to go, places where you can even escape with your children. A man who is physically and emotionally abusive needs help himself, and as a smaller, weaker person, you cannot be the one to help and save him. It is not proof that you don't love him if you remove yourself from danger. Abusive treatment needs to be exposed as the first step to have it stop. It is Satan who seeks to steal from you, kill you, and destroy you (see John 10:10). Living in abuse is neither healthy nor spiritual. Exposing abusive treatment does not apply to our conversation here.

Read the following verses and journal about how they can apply to your public conversation about your husband:

Proverbs 25:9 _Don't betray my husband's confidence_

Matthew 18:15 _Go to him one on one to show his fault, not to others._

Check Yourself

Use the acronym W.A.I.T. to remind you of three questions and one statement that will help you stop this area of corrupt communication about your husband.

Would my husband want others to know this?
Am I angry, or do I honestly need help?
Is the person I'm sharing with a trustworthy, objective counselor or mentor?
Try to work things out between you and your husband.

R.I.S.E. Activity

Radical change. What do I have to radically change when it comes to how I speak to my husband? (List things like your tone of voice, your facial expressions when the two of you are talking, how much you share about your husband's negative traits, etc.)

Corrupt Communication versus Speaking Edifying Words

Tone, nonverbals, impatience.

Initiated by God. How do the following Scriptures apply to what I wrote above in regard to my communication with and/or about my husband?

Ephesians 4:29 No unwholesome talk, should benefit him.

Matthew 12:34 Mouth speaks what heart feels.

1 Peter 2:11-12 What say glorifies God

1 Peter 3:1-2 Submissive, pure, reverent

Philippians 4:8 Say only what true, noble, right, pure, lovely, admirable, excellent, praiseworthy.

Ephesians 5:1-2 Imitate God, live life of love

Proverbs 15:1 Gentle answer turns away wrath. Harsh word stirs anger.

Proverbs 12:18 Reckless words pierce. Wise tongue heals

James 3:5 Great fire set by tongue.

Submission to the Holy Spirit's direction. Considering what God is saying to my heart through the Scriptures above, how is the Holy Spirit directing me to carry out the necessary changes in my communication with my husband?

Tone, attitude

Emergence into full understanding (and readiness to pass the information on). When will I begin living out the necessary lifestyle changes concerning my communication with or about my husband? In what ways am I being led to share my new understanding with those around me? (Perhaps this may start by asking your husband to forgive you.)

Chapter Five

Corrupt Communication versus Speaking Edifying Words: Part Two
To Children

Let no corrupt word proceed out of your mouth, but what is good for necessary edification, that it may impart grace to the hearers. Ephesians 4:29 (NKJV)

Those of us who are mothers can get easily caught up in inflicting damaging put-downs upon our precious children in at least four ways. We put our kids down by what we name them, by directly saying degrading things to them, by comparing our kids to other people's kids, and by comparing our kids to their own brothers and sisters.

Children's Names

When reading through Facebook® recently, I caught this comment:

> My parents thought they were naming me something unique, but really, they just signed me up

for a life with a misspelled, mispronounced, never-finding-on-a-Coke-bottle name.

Personally, I liked this lady's name, and she went on to comment that she grew to like it too; however, my point for this part of the book was being made. Parents, what are we thinking? Some of us are trying to be so cute with our children's names that we could be saddling them with a curse rather than simply with an original moniker. Do we realize that the one word our children will probably hear directed toward them more than any other word is their name? With that in mind, think about what your children are being called every time someone addresses them.

For example, according to closer.co.uk, in an article entitled "Baby Names: 94 of the 'Worst' Names – and their Terrible Meanings," the following top five girls' names sound cute but are problematic: Akuji, Cecilia, Claudia, Deirdre, and Desdemona. Akuji, the only name with which I was not already familiar, is an African name that means "dead and awake." So, if you named your little bundle of joy Akuji, every time you said her name, you would be calling her Little Dead and Awake. You would be saying, "Time for school, Dead and Awake," or "Come to dinner, Dead and Awake," and "Clean your room, Dead and Awake." Not exactly what you want to repeat over and over to a precious little child.

As for those other names on the list: I know a Cecilia, a Claudia, and a Deirdre, and did not realize that I was calling them Blind, Lame, and Sorrowful every time I mentioned their names. And when talking to any

Desdemona, we are saying, "Hi there, Ill-fated, Miserable One, Who is of the Devil."

All is not lost, though, if you named your children something cute that turns out to be associated with a less-than-flattering meaning. Jabez's mother named him a name that means "he will cause pain" because his birth had been so painful. Listening to his name day in and day out could have developed him into a serial killer. However, Jabez operated in opposition to the meaning of his name. He skipped right over what his name meant and prayed to God saying, "Oh, that you would bless me and expand my territory! Please be with me in all that I do and keep me from all trouble and pain" (1 Chronicles 4:9-10 NLT).

I got lucky. I'm pretty sure my mother and father were not looking through baby-name books when I was coming along. My sister was allowed to name me after two of the Mouseketeers Sharon and Annette. My first name, Sharon, means "fertile plain." Little did I know that every time people spoke to me, they were saying, "Hi, Fertile Plain, I'm glad to meet you," or "Fertile Plain, turn in your assignment," and "Fertile Plain, let's go out to dinner." That could have meant I would have been the mother of enough children to have our own football team or orchestra, but the meaning didn't take up residence in me in that direction. As a fertile plain, no wonder my friends tell me I get so much done. All these years, anyone who spoke my name was reaffirming my purpose.

Words have meanings and names are words. One way we can avoid participating in corrupt communication with our children is to start with their names—how we address them, and what we call them every day.

Check Yourself

Look up the meaning of your name and the names of your children, if you have any.

What does your name mean? _Something of great monetary value or a mark of genius_

What do their names mean? _Danny — God is my judge. Tia — joy or happiness._

Consider what people have been calling you, and what you have been calling your children all their lives. Are these positive affirmations? If so, thank God. If not, how can you, like Jabez, redeem the knowledge you now have and determinedly start living in opposition to the negative meaning of your and/or your children's names?

_N/a_

Degrading Comments

I sometimes hear frustrated mothers engaging in this next type of the injurious habit of corrupt communication toward their children when they directly say degrading comments to their kids. Here's the scenario. Mom has either worked or taken care of a couple of toddlers all day. She loads the little ones into their car seats in time for the 3:00 PM run to pick up her elementary-aged son from school. Between the little ones asking a thousand questions and the fourth-grader eager to tell her how much the teacher hates him (and that's why he received the disciplinary note which now requires a parent conference), she's fit to be tied.

I see them when they make what she hopes will be a quick stop at the grocery store. When the two-year-old drops her bunny, the four-year-old steps on it, and the fourth-grader yells at the two-year-old to stop crying like a baby, Mom's had it. She lets loose on the fourth-grader, calling him immature and worthless, and blaming his behavior on a fault she attributes to his father.

Embarrassed, the little boy then does what most kids do when a significant adult puts them down— he stuffs it down inside and he believes it. Despite her assertions at other times that he is "her little man," he is only ten years old, and it is still important to him what adults tell him about himself. The degrading words launched from her frustration carry even heavier weight than her comforting ones when she is calm because of the attached emotions. Subconsciously, this little boy hears the demeaning sentiments from his mother, the most significant woman in his life, and he believes them. After all, she must know the truth about him.

We must be incredibly careful about the words we inflict upon our children. It is painful to be called worthless, stupid, immature, or some derivative thereof. And it is profoundly embarrassing to be the child being cursed at in the store. Children are valuable because God made them. Despite the circumstances of the child's birth, that child is a gift from God and has inestimable worth. Children are also born with intelligence and, as intelligent beings, can be taught, so they are not stupid. Children are indeed immature. That's because they're children. Calling children immature as a put-down demeans the only way they know how to be. When we deem as negative an attribute that children cannot immediately change, we launch a direct attack on their self-esteem. They are deflated and we perpetuate the very problem we are hoping to shame them out of.

"But," you say, "I don't really mean those things. I'm just frustrated."

Well, as the mature adults, it is our responsibility to gain control and say what we mean in a loving way. Dropping frustrated put-downs and replacing them with edifying words that build may seem like a daunting task, but with a little practice—okay, maybe with a lot of practice for some of us—it can be done. We are well-practiced at the way we automatically respond when we're frustrated. We've been reacting to our children this way for years. Perhaps we may even be feeling like we are turning into our mothers—repeating unfavorable words and phrases we used to hear her say. Isn't that scary?

Remember, you want to be a woman God can bless, so the necessary change is worth it and takes a one-two punch: prayer and practice. Proverbs 16:3 tells us "Commit to the LORD whatever you do, and your plans will succeed" (NIV). We must start by praying about our new commitment to use only edifying speech with our children. Then, as we get rid of degrading words, we must next make a conscious effort to fill that vacuum with better responses. Doing this can be as simple as changing a comment like, "Look at what you did! How could you be so stupid?" to "Surely a child as intelligent as you couldn't possibly have thought doing that was a good idea." You see? The act is still discussed as being a problem, but the child is not degraded in the conversation.

Check Yourself

Do you speak words to your children that do not build them up? Are there any ways in which you find yourself verbally degrading your children? In the chart below, list the degrading statements you have heard yourself use, and beside them, list edifying statements you can use instead.

Degrading Statements I've Directed to My Children	Edifying Statements I Can Use Instead

Comparisons to Other People's Children

Another way in which we inflict put-downs upon our children is when we compare them to other people's kids. My son Mark returned from spending the afternoon at the home of one of his friends. He told me his friend's mother loved him. Evidently, Mark was living out the injunction I have always told the boys: "Act even better when you go out so others will know you have some home training."

His friend's mother expressed her admiration by exclaiming, "Look how Mark eats his vegetables. Brian,* why can't you eat your vegetables like Mark does?"

Later she said, "Mark cleared his plate off the table without even being asked. Brian, why can't you remember to bus your plate?"

"Oh Mark, there's no need for you to be so formal. Brian, you could learn a lesson in manners from Mark. He's such a little gentleman."

Needless to say, Brian is not eager to invite Mark back. Although Mark felt flattered (and I must admit I flushed with pride), I had to feel for Brian. In front of his friend, his mother was basically saying something was wrong with him. She was putting his shortcomings on display.

Teenagers don't miss much, and I'm sure Brian was well aware of all Mark was doing that he never did himself. Seeing his mother's sincere appreciation toward Mark's actions would probably have been enough to communicate to Brian that he was lacking in those areas. This may have even made Brian just jealous enough to get his act together. She did not have to punctuate her appreciation with words that demeaned her own son. Sometimes what we don't say speaks louder than what we do say.

If you see great traits in other people's children that you don't see in your own child, work with your child to help him develop the attribute you'd like to see. It's not necessary to point out that you've seen it in someone else.

Also, be sure your circle of friends includes families that share the same values you espouse in your home. This will encourage your child to befriend and hang around kids who exhibit the traits you like. Association breeds assimilation.

Check Yourself

Have you found yourself negatively comparing your child with a friend? If so, you may consider apologizing to your child. You definitely want to change this behavior.

Comparisons to Brothers and Sisters

The final way we will discuss corrupt communication toward a child is the fact that we can put down a child by comparing him with a sibling. My husband pointed out this fault in me recently. I was in a conversation with my friend about our son Matthew's latest accomplishments. I proudly recited how he was on the honor roll, was taking academic trips, was involved in student government, etc. In turn, my friend exclaimed about her daughter's undertakings. We were having quite a lovely Mutual Admiration Society meeting.

So what was the problem? I was doing all this talking within earshot of our son Mark, who is two years younger than Matthew. My husband told me he could see the dejected look on Mark's face, not because I said something bad about him, but because I didn't say anything good. In fact, I didn't say anything at all about him. My conversation was not meant intentionally to exclude or hurt Mark, but neglecting to say anything good implied that he wasn't doing anything worthwhile. It was a put-down of omission and he felt he was being negatively compared to his brother.

Since then, I make it a point to say something positive about both boys whenever I talk about either. I do this when they are present and when they are not. Why? I am practicing filling that vacuum that was left when I decided to change my habit. My boys each have fabulous, unique strengths and talents and I enjoy building them both, whether it's in their presence or in their absence.

A way to find something special about each one of your children is to study their temperaments. I believe this is what is meant by Proverbs 22:6:

> Train up a child in the way he should go, and when he is old he will not depart from it.

The words "train up" mean to "discipline"; the words "the way" mean "course of life"; and the words "he should go" carry with them the idea of an appointment. We are to discipline our children to keep their appointment with the course of life they have been given. Who gives us our destiny? God does. As parents, we have the daunting responsibility of pointing our children toward what God wants them to do with their lives. The only way to know a child's destiny is to know what kind of child we have and watch closely to see what God has placed in him. So, we study our kids' temperaments because God sets this in them at conception.

I have studied both of my boys' temperaments as well as my own. Mark is a sanguine—a playful, fun-loving, charismatic charmer. Matthew is a melancholy/choleric blend—a serious, controlling perfectionist. I'm a choleric/sanguine blend—an optimistic, take-charge leader. I share some traits with my guys but differ in some ways, too. I have to relax my control tendencies when dealing with Mark's laid-back character, and tone down my sense of silliness several notches when faced with Matthew's staunch seriousness. If I were to fault my sons for exhibiting characteristics I don't understand, I would be disobeying Proverbs 22:6. How they act and think is not necessarily because they're wrong, but because they're different. If I am to train them to be what God wants them to be, I have to know how God has designed them as individuals.

We tend to gravitate toward the child whose temperament most complements our own. That's the child we understand and with whom we commiserate, but this leads to favoritism—a huge problem. I found help in two books (that are now out of print but are available online): ***How to Develop Your Child's Temperament*** by Beverly LaHaye (revised and expanded under the title *Understanding Your Child's Temperament*), and ***Raising Christians, Not Just Children*** by Florence Littauer. I highly recommend both books, but if you can't find them, ***Wired That Way***, by Marita and Florence Littauer is a recent release that will give you much of the same great information.

What does all this have to do with speaking words that build? When we know our children well, we can speak words that build them toward what God has destined for them. I can tell my charismatic Mark that he's a leader, people naturally gravitate to him, and that means he must recognize the importance of his actions. He's a role model now and will always be one as he matures into manhood. As he lives obediently before the Lord, his Christian walk will be a light to those around him. If he disobeys, his life will be a detriment as others will follow him down wrong paths. I can build Matthew by encouraging his ability to take charge of situations. He is destined to land in leadership positions which will give him a platform from which he can persuade others toward a relationship with Christ.

God did not give either of our boys their talents to use just for their own enjoyment or success. God trusted them with what He gave them so they could use those gifts for His glory.

Check Yourself

Have you found yourself speaking more favorably about one child over another? Make a list of the positive attributes of the child or children who always seem to come up on the short end of your compliments. Then be sure to affirm their strengths.

Positive Attributes of My Child	Date When I First Affirmed This Attribute

Check Yourself

What are your children's temperaments? Write some specific comments you can use to begin building your children in light of the way God has made them.

Child's Name	Temperament	Comments to Build this Child

R.I.S.E.

Radical change. Regarding speaking favorable words that build to and about my children, what is out of whack in my habits, thoughts, or actions that needs to be radically changed?

_____

_____

Initiated by God. What specific Scriptures are speaking to me about speaking edifying words instead of corrupt communication to and about my children?

Proverbs 12:18 _Reckless words pierce, wise tongue heals_

James 3:5–8 _tongue can't control, can start large fire_

Proverbs 18:21a _of life + death_

Matthew 12:34b–35 _mouth speaks what heart is full of_

Ephesians 6:4 _don't exasperate children, bring up in the Lord_

Proverbs 15:4 _soothing tongue tree of life_

Proverbs 18:4 _words of mouth are deep waters, but fountain of wisdom is a bubbling stream_

Corrupt Communication versus Speaking Edifying Words

Submission to the Holy Spirit's direction. How is the Holy Spirit directing me to carry out the necessary changes regarding how I speak to and about my children?

Only edifying things [handwritten]

Emergence into full understanding (and readiness to pass the information on). Upon making the necessary lifestyle changes in what words come out of my mouth to and about my kids, in what ways am I being led to share my new understanding with those around me?

Chapter Six

Corrupt Communication versus Speaking Edifying Words: Part Three
To Parents, Siblings, and Ex-husbands

Let no corrupt word proceed out of your mouth, but what is good for necessary edification, that it may impart grace to the hearers. Ephesians 4:29

As we continue to talk about how we talk, let's again be reminded of the passage we're studying in this book. Ephesians chapter 4 is comparing our former conduct, the old man who is corrupt, with the renewed person we are becoming. The passage goes on in a very practical way by telling us exactly what we should "put off" and "put on." We are in the midst of the discussion taken up in verse 29 about putting off corrupt communication and putting on communicating edifying words. So, for the past several chapters, we have talked specifically about stopping corrupt communication spoken to those who are probably closest to us: our spouses and our children. We will now talk about communicating with our parents, and then end our discussion of this topic by widening the scope and examining our talk with all people in general. For each of these categories, let's remember we are to "let no corrupt word proceed out of [our] mouth, but what is good for necessary edification, that it may impart grace to the hearers."

Communicating with Parents

God's Word has significant things to say about how we are to relate to our parents. Since we speak to and about them, our Ephesians 4:29 focus verse applies to our words to and about them, so we should be "imparting grace" through our words to our parents. Some of us have amazing, loving parents who provided for our needs, gave ample hugs and kisses, and spoke uplifting messages into our lives on a regular basis. It's no effort at all to speak edifying words to them.

However, I am also aware that not everyone has or had an ideal relationship with her parents. In fact, some families are unfortunately quite painfully broken apart due to the actions of those who brought us into the world. Maybe your mother rarely spoke any uplifting words to you. Perhaps, no matter how you prayed to be Daddy's Little Girl, your father just wasn't there for you for whatever reason. Because of the father-wound, you may have spent years chasing the love of men, only to be crushed over and over again. You may have even been the innocent recipient of shameful abuse. The last thing you want to do is speak to your parents or about your parents in a positive way. If that's you, I hear you, and I want to be sensitive to your mother- and father-wounds I also believe God longs to speak healing to those wounds, and like cocoa butter aids to heal physical wounds and fade physical scars, following God's directive to speak edifying words just could be the miracle drug waiting to be used on those emotional wounds and scars left by parental neglect. Let's see what the Bible says first, and then we'll allow those words to be absorbed into our consciousness and become a reality in our family dynamics.

One of the Ten Commandments speaks directly to our relationship with our parents by saying, "Honor your father and your mother, as the Lord your God has commanded you, that your days may be long, and that it may be well with you in the land which the Lord your God is giving you" (Exodus 20:12 and Deuteronomy 5:16). As you see, God is quite serious about how we ought to view our parents: with honor.

In the Old Testament economy, God assigned very serious consequences for anyone who dishonored his or her parents. For example, anyone who "strikes his father or his mother" and anyone "who curses his father or his mother" was put to death (Exodus 21: 15 and 17). Also, take a look at some other passages showing us God's view on disrespecting parents:

- He who mistreats his father and chases away his mother is a son who causes shame and brings reproach. Proverbs 19:26
- The eye that mocks his father, and scorns obedience to his mother, the ravens of the valley will pick it out, and the young eagles will eat it. Proverbs 30:17

- If a man has a stubborn and rebellious son who will not obey the voice of his father or the voice of his mother, and who, when they have chastened him, will not heed them, then his father and his mother shall take hold of him and bring him out to the elders of his city, to the gate of his city. And they shall say to the elders of his city, 'This son of ours is stubborn and rebellious; he will not obey our voice; he is a glutton and a drunkard.' Then all the men of his city shall stone him to death with stones; so, you shall put away the evil from among you, and all Israel shall hear and fear. Deuteronomy 21:18-21

Thankfully, we no longer live in the Dispensation of Law. We are now living in the Dispensation of Grace (or the Church Age); however, God has not changed since He dictated the Old Testament. His Word transcends all the dispensations because He is immutable; He cannot change. He still commands that we honor our parents, although the punishment for not doing so is not as directly harsh.

Now I can still hear some of you who have experienced profound parental hurt grasping for an excuse to stop reading this chapter. *Surely Jesus couldn't expect for me to show honor toward neglectful and/or abusive parents. The hurts are too deep; the scars too visible.* Be assured that Jesus loves you and He has only your well-being at heart. Because of that, He knows that your deliverance depends upon your obedience on this point.

When speaking to the religious leaders of His day, Jesus used the commandment of honoring one's parents to prove to them that they were honoring God with their lips, but their hearts were far from Him, and their worship was in vain (see Mark 7:6). He exposed how they had created a whole tradition that excused them from the necessity of honoring their parents. Then, over time, they had elevated their tradition to the level of a commandment. By keeping the tradition, they placated themselves into believing they were doing what God would have them do. In Mark 7:9-13 (NKJV), Jesus reveals their folly:

> He said to them, "*All too* well you reject the commandment of God, that you may keep your tradition. For Moses said, 'Honor your father and your mother'; and, 'He who curses father or mother, let him be put to death.' But you say, 'If a man says to his father or mother, "Whatever profit you might have received from me *is* Corban"—'(that is, a gift *to God*), then you no longer let him do anything for his father or his mother, making the Word of God of no effect through your tradition which you have handed down. And many such things you do."

So as gently as possible, I'm trying to communicate that no matter how we were treated by our parents, God's directive to us is to honor them. So how? How can we speak edifying words—words that impart grace—to our parents?

If Parents Are Living or Have Passed On and Were Positive

The word "honor" used in Exodus 20:12 means "to make weighty or rich." In other words, our verbal utterances to and about our parents should show them serious respect. It takes knowing and understanding people to show them honor. Even though we are well aware that our dads and moms were fallible, and we had occasional disagreements, those who had parents who were positive role models and loving, self-denying human beings, find it easy to speak of them fondly and respectfully. We easily give them a pass for the times they blew it (in our eyes), because in the grand scheme of things, we can tell they were really trying to do their best on our behalf. Dads who were home regularly, worked to supply for the family's needs, loved Mom, supported us at school events, dispensed fair discipline, and put Christ first automatically earn our love and respect. Moms who made the house a home, kissed away hurts, listened to our problems, offered wise counsel, and added fun to our lives get all the kudos we can muster.

As these parents age, we honor them by reminiscing with them about the great job they did in their parenting role. Laugh with them about how their discipline helped even though you didn't understand it at the time. Tell the stories from your point of view and listen (again and again if necessary) to the stories from their perspective. I always enjoy recounting the story (in the company of others, of course) of when Mark ran away from home, and I love to see how embarrassed he gets hearing it! It amazes me to hear that his recollection of the incident really isn't that different from mine. I also get a huge kick out of hearing my boys tell me or others about childhood incidents involving me that they remember. Sometimes I'm surprised by their admissions of things I did not know, but usually, it's just fun to hear their memories.

Something else that honors aging parents are regular phone calls, cards, and letters. All three say, "I was thinking of you just now." A phone call produces a smile in the present; cards and letters produce smiles that keep on coming because those messages are tangibly relived every time they are read again (and they are read over and over again).

If our parents have moved into eternity, the pain of their loss eventually begins to be replaced with the comfort of precious memories as we share positive stories about them with others. Whether our wonderful parents are living or dead, we edify them and impart grace as we keep their memory alive in the positive words about them that we share. The lessons we learned and influence of their lives pass from us to a new generation as we continue to talk fondly of them.

Check Yourself

Share with your group (or journal if you are doing this study on your own) an especially fond childhood memory you have of your father, your mother, and/or the main parental figure who raised you.

_____

_____

_____

_____

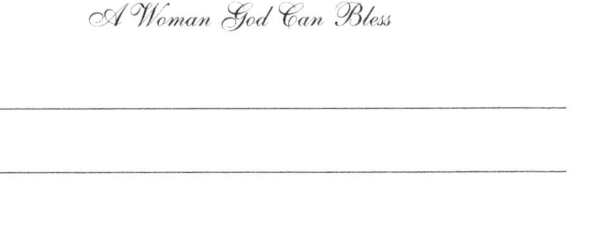

<u>If Parents Are Living or Dead and Were Negative</u>

Now to the hard category. What if one's parents were negative models of parenting? How in heaven's name are we expected to show them honor with our words when, in all honesty, they were raunchy human beings? My friend J. Rae* shares how the Lord has worked in her difficult relationship with her mother:

> It's painful for me to talk about my mother. Yes, she's still alive, to date she is ninety-nine, and, and complains as much now as she ever has … By age ten and eleven, I began to realize "My mommy isn't like other mommies." I realized mine was older than everyone else's, and that mine was angry a lot of the time, or if not outright angry and screaming, she was very tense or anxious.
>
> My mother was German and a war bride, and it was years before I realized I had been raised by a person with pretty severe PTSD, along with anger issues, bitterness, and an overall complaining sweeping negativity to her every perspective. Her temperament was volatile and un-

predictable. Her "go to" response to everything was "NO!" or anger, or fear that instantly went into anger. She deeply believed and constantly said, "Don't hope for things, and then you won't be disappointed when they don't happen." She was astonishingly critical of everyone and everything, and very jealous and envious of others. Nothing was ever good enough …

I became an overachiever in school, drove myself to get straight As in everything, striving to be the perfect child so she would be happy with me…

It took until I was in my forties to begin to get insights into my mom, because I was now a full-grown woman myself. With much prayer God gave me more understanding of how much going through the war in Germany had affected her, and to also understand that she had grown up in old-world Germany being influenced by an extremely harsh culture…

My mom has continued to be incredibly unkind to me, intentionally critical, especially when my dad was dying of Alzheimer's… She did and said things to me that were unspeakably crushing, but God was so alive in my heart telling me, "Do NOT get sucked into her black hole… Your father's life and salvation are both on the line here, you MUST keep your focus on ME because you are the only voice of faith and love, you are the only light that I can use to reach your dad".

People have asked me so many times "Why have you always continued to reach out to your mom? Why are you still so loving when she abuses you, doesn't celebrate you, and insults you so?" I have deeply believed that the Word calls me to honor her, and Jesus says in John 14 that those who love Him keep His Word, keep His commands. It isn't based on a feeling; it's based on wanting to honor HIM. If I had based my "relationship" with my mom on how I felt, I would have stopped seeing her by the time I was thirty for sure, if not earlier.

I asked the Lord a question once when I was especially crushed afresh by my mom's ability to be so cruel and disrespectful. I was weeping and asked Him "Why did you ever choose her to be my mother?" The answer that came back to my heart gave me a real solace. He said, "I gave you to her as a GIFT. Your energy, laughter, exuberance, playful humor, silliness, strength, outbursts of song were all to bring her joy." It felt wonderful to hear the heavenly Father tell my heart that His plan had been for me to be a gift, she just didn't know how to trust or enjoy me that way… Again, for me it comes down to living for an audience of One and trusting that He is working things out for His best purposes. The

Lord deserves glory, honor, and praise whether things are going the way we hope for or not, because He is God, and that is reason enough!

Obviously, the best case scenario would be for you to be able to share your hurts with your parents and hear them admit their mistakes, accept responsibility for their actions, and sincerely apologize. If offending parents are still living, there is always a possibility of this development taking place. Hallelujah! May this be the case for many!

However, what if living parents who were neglectful, abusive, or who came up short in some other way refuse to face their faults and acknowledge our hurts? And what if those parents have died without giving us the opportunity to hear an apology and be reconciled? First, determine to be true to your new dedication to obey Ephesians 4:29 and "let no corrupt word proceed out of your mouth, but what is good for necessary edification, that it may impart grace to the hearers." Once you have determined to obey God's Word on this issue, here are six steps to move you into the realization of that goal: redefine, redesign, realign, reassign, re-enshrine, and recline.

Redefine – In order to obey God's Word and set up the atmosphere to be able to honor neglectful and/or abusive parents, it is necessary to redefine the way you see yourself. To do that, start by facing the reality of your past, and then believe this new truth: what happened in your past does not have to define your present nor derail your future. In an October 3, 2011 *Psychology Today* article, Dr. Mark Banschick, M.D. states:

> You … don't want to be stuck in that wound and have it define your entire future. Maybe the best you can do is grieve the fact that this terrible event touched your life. Maybe you have to wrestle with this issue with God, Himself. That is up to you.
>
> But, in the absence of forgiveness, grief can still work. Life is not fair and you were terribly hurt. Go through the mourning process. Grieve the innocent boy, girl, man or woman who had been injured so badly. Allow yourself to experience the anger, the hurt, and the despair of grief—but work towards acceptance; an acceptance that is tempered by memory. This is not a happy acceptance; aim towards a meaningful acceptance that acknowledges that there is a lot about life that is not in our control.

What happened to you as a child was not your fault. Acknowledge it so you can deal with it but stop allowing it to characterize you.

Redesign – You are an adult now. You get to decide what your life will be like. Remodel the old house of your memories. Your past will never change, but like an old, familiar house that has been remodeled, the renovation of your reactions toward those memories will make living with them bearable. And if you give

God a chance, He can turn those remade "rooms" into functioning places where others can learn to overcome just as you did by visiting with you and listening to your deliverance story.

Realign – You can exchange the power your parents had over you with the power of Christ. "So humble yourselves under the mighty power of God, and at the right time he will lift you up in honor. Give all your worries and cares to God, for he cares about you"

1 Peter 5:6- 8 (NLT). "Take My yoke upon you and learn from Me," says Christ, "for I am gentle and lowly in heart, and you will find rest for your souls" (Matthew 11:29).

Re-assign – You can take control of your life and your reactions. Once you have redesigned by taking the reins of your life back, you can reassign the real definitions to what happened in your life. Step away from denial.

Barrett and Trepper's predictable stages of denial are as follows:

1. Denial of facts: ("It never happened; you're a liar!"), followed by:
2. Denial of awareness: ("I was drunk," or "I didn't realize I was neglecting you; you should have told me"), followed by:
3. Denial of responsibility: ("You were the one who was seductive," or "If your mother didn't deny me, I wouldn't have to have turned to you."), and finally:
4. Denial of impact: ("It only happened a few times," or "It was only fondling," or "OK, so I beat

you. Why do you always have to dwell on the past? You're just too sensitive; get over it!").

Look at your past honestly, but with a distance like that of thumbing through a family photo album. Painful memories not denied become sources of celebration over what you have learned, how far you have come, and what a friend you have in Jesus for helping you survive.

Re-enshrine—Allow God to reign where He belongs, in the preeminent place in your life, that space that had been reserved for your bitterness. Return to church and Bible study. You have taken the first step by reading this book. Now dive into the Word of God, seeing His wisdom as the primary authority over every other word spoken to you. Look to God to be the healer of your emotional pain.

Recline – Now you are free to forgive. You can rest free of bitterness and free of having the past hold you down. In her book, *Do Yourself a Favor: Forgive*, Joyce Meyer says, "Staying angry at someone who has hurt you is like taking poison and hoping that your enemy will die. Our unforgiveness hurts us more than it does anyone else." One of my friends recently showed me how this forgiveness works.

Arneda traveled out of town recently to try to get her elderly father's affairs in order. She went to a lot of trouble in trying to understand what he was supposed to be receiving in Medicare benefits and social security income. Things got even more confusing as she tried to unravel the mess he had made of his bills. There were even other people trying to lay claim on his money.

Arneda's concern for her dad seems appropriate, something any loving daughter would do, right? I agree, until you understand that her dad had been much less than the model father throughout her entire childhood. Absent from her life (although she knew who and where he was), unfaithful to her mother (his wife), and neglectful of their needs, this man had broken every promise, and had shattered his little daughter's dreams and securities over and over again. Yet, here she was taking care of his needs when he had never taken care of hers.

I asked Arneda how she could do this. Her answer: because he's my father. She said, "Who am I to judge what he deserves? I just know what God expects of me. If Momma was still alive, I probably wouldn't have gone to take care of his affairs out of loyalty to her. She was never able to drop her bitterness and I would have felt obligated to be on her side. After Momma died, I felt free to be able to openly follow my conscience regarding how I should deal with my dad, so I had to go see about him. It was the right thing—the Christian thing—to do."

Check Yourself

If you were raised in a dysfunctional environment, you may not know what a functional relationship between parent and child looks like.

1. If your parents are alive or dead, and you have or had a great relationship with them, share with your group some reasons why your relationship works or worked. Focus on the traits that make the relationship flourish more than on the story. (For example: Respecting each other's space—even with our insistence that she was welcome any time, my mother would not just pop up at my house once I got married. And we would not just assume she was always available to babysit. We would respect her calendar and ask weeks in advance if she would be free and if she wanted to care for the kids when we wanted to go out.)
2. If your parents are alive and you have a difficult relationship with one or both of them:
   a. Start praying about opportunities to build your relationship.
   b. Pray about what needs to be discussed in order to be healed.
   c. Pray about what can just be forgiven.
   d. Look for opportunities to honor your parents, then act out those opportunities.
3. If your parents were difficult and have passed away:
   a. Admit the hurt you endured from your parents.
   b. Confess your lingering anger to God.
   c. Write a letter to your parents explaining all your feelings and then let them know that you have asked God to help you let the pain

go. List what you have learned from the hurts and how you will let God turn each of the hurts into something that can help someone else.

Communicating with Siblings

One would think that speaking words that "impart grace to" parents, siblings, and extended family members should be the easiest thing in the world to do. After all, these are people who should be close to us, people we love. However, it's those closest to us who know most readily just exactly how to push our buttons and dance around on our last nerve.

This truth is illustrated best in Scripture via the account of the life of Joseph, Jacob's (Israel 's) favorite son. I'll abbreviate the tale here, but I recommend that you read the whole story in Genesis chapters 37– 50 to get all the twists and turns.

In brief, (okay now, try to keep up), through a series of crooked events, Jacob (Joseph's dad) ended up with two wives, Leah and Rachel; two concubines, Bilhah and Zilpah; twelve sons, and one daughter. The last two sons, Joseph and Benjamin, were born to him by his favorite wife, Rachel, so her first son, Joseph, was Jacob's favorite.

You needed that backstory to understand the severity of the jealously that the ten half-brothers felt toward Joseph. Every one of them outranked Joseph in line for their father's inheritance. Still, Jacob actively showed favoritism to Joseph. That favoritism, and

Joseph's poor timing in sharing with his brothers his dreams of his brothers bowing down to him, got him bullied to the point of getting him sold into slavery by his brothers. The brothers then told their father Jacob an abominable lie that Joseph had been killed and eaten by a wild animal. No more bragging troublemaker

But not so fast. Joseph was very much alive and well. He went through multiple problems in Egypt but kept landing on his feet because God kept blessing him. He ended up interpreting the Pharaoh's troubling dream about a coming famine, being promoted to Vice Pharaoh, and being placed in charge of doling out food during the crisis .

Enter Joseph's brothers. There they were, the ten who had sold him and counted him as dead, asking to buy food, bowing down to him as the Vice Pharaoh, not realizing they were in the presence of their very own brother. At that very moment, Joseph had a decision to make. Would he send those ten to be killed for what they had done to him, or would he respond in the character of the righteous, God-fearing, God-honoring man he had been since he arrived in this strange land?

His brothers were scared spitless when they realized this Vice Pharaoh really was their brother. They expected to get what they deserved, but Joseph did the right thing. He honored God by forgiving his brothers, noticing that God had used what they meant for evil as the very move that ended up saving their whole family. God's directive to refuse to let a "corrupt word proceed out of your mouth" applies to speaking to your siblings, too. Proverbs 18:19 says, "A brother who has been insulted is harder to win back than a walled city, and arguments separate people like the barred gates of a palace" (NCV).

Check Yourself

1. Are you able to speak honorably to your brothers and sisters who have hurt you? If not, why not?

   N/A

   _____

2. What is your plan to build a bridge over the gap between you and your siblings?

   _____

   _____

Communicating with Ex-husbands

Again, best case scenario: admit his mistakes, accept responsibility for his actions, and sincerely apologize. This is probably another whole book in itself. We'll deal with the bitterness that accompanies divorce in chapter 11. Suffice it here to say that when it comes to communication with your ex-husband, God's sentiment about communication is no different than it is for any other interaction. Put a guard on your mouth. Speak like a kingdom woman even to your ex-husband. Do not let the aggravation of your situation change your righteousness.

R.I.S.E.

Radical change. What is out of whack in my habits, thoughts, or actions related to my parents, siblings, and/or ex-husband that needs to be radically changed?

Initiated by God. What is Scripture telling me about:

    a. How I should relate to my parents?
    b. How I should relate to my siblings?
    c. How I should relate to my ex-husband?

Submission to the Holy Spirit's direction. How is the Holy Spirit directing me to carry out the necessary changes in my relationship with my parents, siblings, and ex-husband?

Emergence into full understanding (and readiness to pass the information on). Upon making the necessary lifestyle changes, in what ways am I being led to share with those around me about my new understanding of my relationship with my parents, my siblings, and my ex-husband?

Chapter Seven

Corrupt Communication versus Speaking Edifying Words: Part Four Communicating with Friends and Strangers-- Gossip, Cursing, Apologetics

Let no corrupt word proceed out of your mouth, but what is good for necessary edification, that it may impart grace to the hearers. Ephesians 4:29

Ok, so we have talked for the past three chapters about the contrast between and the importance of speaking corrupt communication and speaking edifying words. We ought to be convinced by now that our tongues can be lethal weapons or agents of extraordinary blessing, and women whom God can bless know how to emphasize the latter use.

With all that said, three obvious issues dealing with our mouths must be addressed in this discussion. We will not spend a long time on any particular one; just enough to spin the spotlight on the eyes of our hearts. Each of us women who are determined to be women God can bless must determine how much time we need to spend breaking the first two habits and building the third. These three issues are gossip, cursing, and apologetics.

Gossip

The first question I asked myself when approaching this section of the book was the obvious: so, what does the Bible say about gossip? We all know gossip is bad, everybody at church tells us it's bad, but I wanted to give my readers the real, solid lowdown. As I started to comb through the twenty-five-plus verses about gossip, I landed upon a website entitled *Going by Faith*. The writer of the blog, a woman who only goes by the name Jenn, had basically done all my work for me. She wrote a beautiful blog that not only talks about the Bible verses but separates them into eight easy-to-understand categories. Since it's a waste of time to reinvent the wheel, here in abbreviated form is Jenn's astute breakdown of what God's Word says about gossip. (For Jenn's full blog post, see http://goingbyfaith.com/types-of-gossip/)

1. Slander: spreading rumors or lies about a person to cause damage *purposely*. James 4:11
2. Dishing: sharing the "juicy info" you learned about someone. Proverbs 20:19

3. Rumors: [The information is] not good, and it's also not confirmed as true, but you tell someone or ask someone else about it to get more information. Proverbs 13:3
4. Backbiting: speaking spiteful or slanderous words about another who is not present and can do nothing in defense. It's secretive. Proverbs 25:23
5. Not-Really-Joking Jokes: [taking] part of the truth and turning it into a joke about someone that makes others question that person's character. Proverbs 21:24
6. Planting Seeds: gossip is said in such a way to make the listener question or assume something about the character of a person. James 3:5, Proverbs 16:28
7. Whispered Innuendo: [you] make subtle insinuations that can mislead others into thinking wrong thoughts. Proverbs 26:20
8. Got-This-All-Wrong Gossip: you probably got it wrong, but spread it anyway. James 4:17

Check Yourself

So, who's guilty? Have you been gossiping? Which type(s) of gossip has/have been your problem? Why do you think you participated in each case of gossip you identified? What are you going to do to be sure you will not gossip again? Do you owe someone an apology?

Cursing

When most of us first read the first phrase of Ephesians 4:29, we probably immediately thought it referred only to cursing. "Let no corrupt word proceed out of your mouth …" But as we've seen, corrupt communication is much more far-reaching. Still, let's not ignore the obvious.

To curse is to detest utterly; abhor; abominate, imprecate evil upon; damn; denounce. When we curse someone, we are declaring the ultimate put-down on that person. We want them to go away, be hurt, feel small, and know that they are unworthy. The words of our mouths are only supposed to flow forth in order to build the other person up.

Even our ejaculations of pain need not be curse words. My students could not believe me when in a conversation about cursing one day, I said I did not curse. My explanation included the fact that I never heard my parents curse, so curse words simply were not a part of my vocabulary. They continued to badger me and finally figured they had me with the challenge, "What do you say when you hit your toe on a table leg? You can't be thinking about God then." My answer, "I say ouch!"

I believe as Christians, we ought to strive to be above reproach. In the area of cursing, that means we don't simply substitute milder words for the more recognizable common curse words, but we revolutionize our whole way of reacting. Instead of regurgitating our anger or frustration or disgust verbally, we can answer as kingdom women. After all, "A soft answer turns away wrath, but a harsh word stirs up anger" (Proverbs 15:1). Also consider that God's Word tells us, "Out of the same mouth proceed blessing and cursing. My brethren, these things ought not to be so" (James 3:10 NKJ).

Check Yourself

Are you a woman who curses? Are you willing to turn your mouth over to the Lord? When He purchased your salvation, He bought all of you with His blood. Your body as His temple includes your mouth and vocal cords. Make the decision today to allow God to clean up your cursing, replacing those words with a completely new manner of responding to every perturbing situation or conversation.

Apologetics

What is apologetics? Apologetics is "reasoned arguments or writings in justification of something," and in our case, that 'something' is the Christian faith.

All believers are commanded to go into all the world and preach the gospel (see Matthew 28:19). We do not all have to be seminary graduates in order to tell people the good news of the gospel. We just need to tell people about the love of God through Jesus Christ. If we do that regularly, we're good. However, if we're not participating in apologetics, or we are doing it incorrectly, then we are participating in corrupt communication.

Just like a lie is just as much what you do say as what you don't say, so apologetics is just as much what you do say as what you don't say. In other words, if I tell someone the wrong things about Jesus, I have done apologetics wrong. And if I refuse or neglect to talk about Jesus when I should do so, I have done apologetics wrong as well.

Let me explain with an example. I get my nails done at Candy Nails. The woman who owns the shop, Candy, hails from Vietnam and practices the Buddhist faith. She's friendly and runs a tight ship, making sure all the ladies keep the shop sparkling clean and sanitary. She also makes sure her operators remain current and aware of all the new health and beauty trends as pertain to nail and skin care. Candy also has a genius business mind, owning several other businesses besides the nail shop.

Since I've been a customer for over eighteen years, Candy and I have become a little better associated than her average customers. From time to time, she shares personal thoughts with me. I have prayed for opportunities to share Christ with her, still respecting her beliefs and her culture.

Candy shared with me one day that she uses much of her money to help poor people in Vietnam. She avoids humanitarian organizations and touches people herself. She uses her relatives still living there to identify the neediest people or families in their town. Then several times a year, she goes to Vietnam to fulfill the needs of those people. She does things like take truckloads of food and replace a lean-to with a cinderblock home on a foundation with a real roof. The pictures are amazing, but her story took a strange twist. As she finished showing me the photos, she said, "But I still feel empty. I'm doing all of this, but why do I still feel empty?"

My heart jumped. God just served me a scrumptious plate full of apologetic moment. I could have just nodded my head and then insured her that she had nothing to feel bad about. She was doing good deeds and should be proud of herself. Letting this moment pass without giving her the God-answer she needed would have been a misuse of apologetics.

Or I could have done what I did. I seized the moment. First, I commended her. What she was doing was wonderful. It was much more than many business owners do who own much larger businesses than hers. Then I shared with Candy that she may have felt empty because God was not her reason for doing what she did. "As a Christian," I said, "I get a deep sense of peace and fulfillment when I do the things my God wants me to do. When I visit the sick or fulfill someone's needs, I do it because of and in the name of Jesus Christ who is the God I serve. You see, my benevolence is to please my God, not my own self. My actions please Him, and in turn, He blesses me, so I can feel fulfilled rather than empty."

She took this all in and I feel that God used me to at least plant a seed in Candy's heart that may one day grow large enough to push Buddhism out of the way so that the love of Christ can spread throughout her life. All of the operators in Candy's shop are not Buddhist; some are protestant Christians, and some are Catholic. I pray for them, that they get opportunities to share Christ with Candy, too.

Check Yourself

Anyone who crosses your path is a prime candidate for a conversation with you about Jesus. Who crosses your path regularly who has not heard about Jesus from you? Write their names here, pray for an open door the next time you see them, and brainstorm as to how you can interject the gospel message of Jesus Christ into your next encounter.

People who regularly cross my path whom I do not know well.	Prayer and brainstorm about how to interject Jesus into the next situation.
Hint: hair stylist, grocery store clerk, gas station attendant, mailman, child's teacher, etc.	

R.I.S.E.

Radical change. What is out of whack in my habits, thoughts, or actions regarding gossiping and cursing that needs to be radically changed? What needs to be changed regarding my participation in apologetics?

Initiated by God. What is Scripture telling me about:

    a. Gossip?
    b. Cursing?
    c. Apologetics?

Submission to the Holy Spirit's direction. How is the Holy Spirit directing me to:

   a. Stop gossiping?
   b. Stop cursing?
   c. Start speaking up with apologetic comments and/or answers when conversations leave openings for me to insert Jesus?

Emergence into full understanding (and readiness to pass the information on). Upon making the necessary lifestyle changes, in what ways am I being led to share with those around me my new understanding of gossip, cursing, and apologetics?

Chapter Eight

Lying versus Speaking the Truth

Therefore, putting away lying, "*Let* each one *of you* speak truth with his neighbor," for we are members of one another. Ephesians 4:25

We have spent the last four chapters putting off corrupt communication and putting on speaking edifying words. Our transformation into women God can bless must include tackling one more issue dealing with our mouths: lying versus speaking the truth. In our Ephesians chapter 4 passage, verse 25 says, "Therefore, putting away lying, 'Let each one of you speak truth with his neighbor,' for we are members of one another."

Notice that the words "Let each one of you speak truth with his neighbor" are in quotation marks in this verse. If you remember English class in school, one use of quotations marks means the writer is quoting or restating the words contained within. Those words were uttered by someone. Paul is quoting words that were spoken by God as reported by the Old Testament prophet Zechariah. In a discussion about how God would bless His people once they turned back to Him, Zechariah reports that God says this is how His people will act. One of the things His restored and forgiven people would do would be to speak truth. The verse says:

> These *are* the things you shall do:
> Speak each man the truth to his neighbor;
> Give judgment in your gates for truth, justice, and peace.
> (Zechariah 8:16)

So, in quoting Zechariah, Paul is giving validation to the things he's telling us we should do. When His people check themselves and are returned to God's graces—or "straighten up and fly right," as my mother used to say—the natural result is a change in actions. In this place in our discussion, one of those changes in action is a change in how we relate verbally with our neighbors. We stop lying and speak the truth.

Do we lie? Do Christians lie? Unfortunately, the people of God do lie. How do we know God's people lie? Because God's Word has to tell us not to do so. God's Word is written for God's people, so God knows that we have to be told to stop doing the sins in which we are involved.

So, if we are to speak the truth to our neighbors, several questions need to be answered. First, what is truth? Second, who is my neighbor? Third, how have I been lying to my neighbor in the first place?

First, what is truth? This question was put to Jesus while He stood before Pilate the night before His crucifixion. Jesus had been arrested and taken to Pilate so that Pilate would sentence Him to death. Although the people kept shouting for Jesus' death, Pilate was disturbed. He couldn't justify a death sentence and he didn't want Jesus' blood on his hands. To try to figure things out, Pilate took Jesus into a private room and began to interrogate Him. (See John chapter 18). Pilate asked, "Are You the King of the Jews?", "Am I a Jew?", "What have You done?", and, "Are You a king, then?" Jesus responded to each of Pilate's questions.

To that last question, Jesus answered, "You say rightly that I am a king. For this cause I was born, and for this cause I have come into the world, that I should bear witness to the truth. Everyone who is of the truth hears My voice."

This answer rocked Pilate's world. He was the one in the position to pass out truth in *his* judgments and have people listen to *his* voice. Yet here, this itinerate preacher about whom he'd obviously heard some amazing things, was clearly telling him that only those who are "of the truth" hear His voice.

Matthew Henry's commentary explains that "of the truth" means:

> The subjects of [Christ's kingdom] are those that are *of the truth*. All that by the grace of God are rescued from under the power of the father of lies, and are disposed to receive the truth and submit to the power and influence of it, will hear Christ's voice, will become his subjects, and will bear faith and true allegiance to Him … All that are in love with truth will hear the voice of Christ … so that, by *hearing Christ's voice*, we

know that we are *of the truth* (Matthew Henry's Commentary, John 18:37 emphasis added).

Not only did Pilate seem to understand that Jesus was challenging whether or not he was "of the truth," it is clear that Pilate understood Jesus' meaning of the phrase "hear My voice." The word "hear" is the Greek word *akoúō* which means "to hear God's voice which prompts Him to birth faith within." It is the same word which is used in Romans 10:17, "So then faith comes by hearing, and hearing by the Word of God." This Romans verse is saying that faith is born in us through the ear gate when, through physically hearing God's Word, our hearts spiritually hear, thus awakening our understanding to our connection with God. Without said awakening, we remain dead in our trespasses and sins.

So, Pilate understood Jesus to be saying, "Yes, not only am I a king, I am The King who has a following of people who understand truth that exceeds your knowledge and power. You can only know this truth if you too are one of my followers."

Pilate was looking for Jesus to plead His own case for release and talk His way out of the predicament He was in. Instead, Jesus' words seemed to awaken an awareness in Pilate that the tables had turned. Jesus had a release— the truth in question— to offer him. Pilate's next utterance was the immediate involuntary reaction to Jesus's challenge.

"What is truth?" Pilate interjected in John 18:38.

The truth Jesus had spoken of in verse 37 was the Greek word alétheia meaning "truth, but not merely truth as spoken; truth of idea, reality, sincerity, truth in the moral sphere, divine truth revealed to man, straightforwardness." After asking about *that* truth, Pilate left the room and never got Jesus' answer. If he had heard "truth in the moral sphere" and "divine truth revealed to man," it would have been impossible to keep his position in the Roman government and rule that Jesus should be crucified. Pilate would have been personally obligated to admit that Jesus was king, not Caesar. And for Pilate, that would have been political suicide.

Check Yourself

Are you clear on the truth that Jesus Christ is God, the King of kings, the Lord of lords, the second Person of the Trinity, God the Son? YES NO

Write these verses in your own words to understand the truth of who Jesus is:

John 20:27–28

Proof of crucifixion – wound marks

Colossians 2:8–9

Deity of Christ lived in bodily form.

John 1:1 and 14

Word ver's God. Word became flesh

Philippians 2:5-6

Be like Jesus. He became us, humble himself self for us.

2 Peter 1:1

Servant of Christ

John 10:30

Jesus + Father are one.

Lying versus Speaking the Truth

(If questions still exist concerning the identity of Jesus, start a conversation with your study group or visit your pastor to receive a clear understanding.)

So, as the discussion and verses above indicate, the answer to the question, "What is truth?" is simple. Jesus is the answer. God is the truth, God has the truth, and God speaks the truth. If we are His followers, we are people "of the truth," and therefore, must be people who speak truth as well.

Now that we have established the definition of truth and a determination to add being a truth-speaker to our to-do list, we need to tackle the question, "Who is my neighbor?" Who is the person to whom I am not obligated to tell the truth?

The game show *To Tell the Truth* comes to mind. On this show, three people are presented to a panel of four celebrity judges. Each one introduces himself as the same name. Then the host reads a short biography explaining that person's interesting or odd job. By asking a series of questions, the panel must guess which person is actually the true one the biography describes. Only the real individual is sworn to tell the truth; the other two try to fool the panel.

We are the real guest and the celebrity panel represents our neighbor who must listen and watch us to see if we are who we say we are. Since all we do and say is a never-ending-until-we-die episode, by this scenario, we can understand that anyone we come in contact with is our neighbor. Our lives are living epistles, letters about what God is like, being read every moment of every day. So, our words must be words of truth to any and every one.

In chapter 57 of Philip Graham Ryken's book *Exodus: Saved for God's Glory,* from his Preaching the Word series, the author sums up our discussion by quoting the great theologian, John Calvin, and then giving his own final words. Ryken writes:

> John Calvin summarized the biblical teaching [on truth telling] as follows: "The purpose of this commandment is: since God (who is truth) abhors a lie, we must practice truth without deceit toward one another." Honesty really is the best policy, not simply because it helps us get along with other people, but because our interpersonal communication ought to be grounded in the character of God.[1]

Before we continue, let's just have one quick word about speaking the truth in love. Whenever there is a conversation among Christians about confrontation, someone brings up the partial verse and says, "But you know, it's important to 'speak the truth in love.'" We say this to each other in an effort to soften the blow of a harsh message; however, although this comment is well-intentioned, it is being quoted out of context.

Ephesians 4:15, which says, "But, speaking the truth in love, may grow up in all things into Him who is the head—Christ" is the second part of a previous thought. In his admonition to us to "walk worthy," this is talking

---

[1] Ryken, P. G., & Hughes, R. K. (2005). *Exodus: Saved for God's Glory* (p. 659). Wheaton, IL: Crossway Books.

about speaking the truth about our faith. It is not talking about how we speak to people in general. Yes, we should speak kindly to one another, but this verse does not teach us that.

From the beginning of Ephesians chapter 4, Paul is instructing us on how to "walk worthy of the calling with which [we] were called" (Ephesians 4:1). He goes on to tell us to be like Christ. To accomplish that goal, he informs that Christ gave leaders to the church to equip the saints for ministry and encourage them while they work toward unity. Instead of being tossed around as immature children during this process, we should grow in Christ together by "speaking the truth in love" to one another.

So you see, the context of "speaking the truth in love" has to do with speech related to how to live as a Christian. We are to encourage each other, in the most loving way possible, to live as we ought to live. In doing so, sometimes subjects have to be breached that are uncomfortable. We may need to challenge a lifestyle choice or a decision being made by another believer and approaching that individual may be awkward. Still, we are admonished to do so with a loving attitude rather than an accusatory or judgmental one.

We are to be kind as we speak to and relate to one another in general, but this verse is not the one teaching that to us.

The universal teaching of the Bible is to love God and love one another. Romans 12:10 tells us to "love each other with genuine affection and take delight in honoring each other" (NLT). And when asked to tell the greatest commandment, Jesus answered, "You shall love the Lord your God with all your heart, with all your soul, and with all your mind.' This is the first and great commandment. And the second is like it: 'You shall love your neighbor as yourself.' On these two commandments hang all the Law and the Prophets" (Matthew 22:37-40).

So, be kind and tell the truth to each other.

Truth with our Equals

Are we speaking the truth to others? Let's start by thinking of those who are our equals, people who are not our superiors or people who are responsible to us. For me, these are the easiest people with whom to be honest. I have nothing to win or lose by lying to them. In fact, being completely honest tends to strengthen these relationships. I can think of two of my friends in particular with whom I can share my innermost feelings, thoughts, and secrets. They share their issues with me as well. We joke with each other that we must remain close friends because we both know too much. And the things we've shared with each other will go to our graves with us unless the originator decides to tell it.

We all need someone, at least one secret-sharing-ride-or-die girlfriend who will be there in a pinch. Songs through the ages have been written about this. They keep us real; they keep our feet on the ground and our heads out of the clouds. When I'm thinking more of myself than I ought to think, one of them can pull my coattail and remind me of my humanity. To the contrary, when I'm singing the blues and wallowing in thinking less of myself, one of those ladies will lift me from the dumps. And in both instances, I can and do return the favor. We can say anything to each other and not be judged, misunderstood, or thrown under the bus.

Check Yourself

Consider the following verses. Journal or discuss with your group times you have lived through a situation when you were on the giving or receiving end of what the verse is talking about.

- Faithful are the wounds of a friend,
  But the kisses of an enemy are deceitful. Proverbs 27:6

- A friend loves at all times,
  And a brother is born for adversity. Proverbs 17:17

- "To him who is afflicted, kindness should be shown by his friend,
  Even though he forsakes the fear of the Almighty. Job 6:14

- Greater love has no one than this, than to lay down one's life for his friends. John 15:13

Truth with Those for Whom we are Responsible (kids, employees, volunteers)

Are we speaking the truth to those for whom we are responsible? As the parent or boss, we hold quite a lot of sway over those for whom we are responsible. Our careless or wrong actions could mean their lives or livelihoods. If we expect to receive respect from them, it is imperative that we are honest with them.

It can seem innocuous to tell little lies to our children, especially when they are toddlers; however, that's a bad habit to start. We won't want them to lie to us when they grow up, so we shouldn't use lying as an easy alternative when an honest answer is uncomfortable. There is always an age-appropriate, honest answer that can be given. We can also honestly tell our children that we don't know the answer or that we are uncomfortable talking about that at the time. If the child asks about a particularly sensitive issue, perhaps someone else in the family would be a better person to answer the question.

My youngest son Mark was about five or six years old when he asked to go to the park one day. I said, "We'll see."

As he turned to leave, his dejected remark was, "We'll see means 'no.'"

Teaching moment!

"Wait, Mark," I said. "Come back. I didn't say no."

"Well, whenever you say that, we don't get to do it."

"It only seems that way, Mark. Sometimes when I say, "We'll see," we do end up doing what you asked. But tell me this: what happens when I say yes?"

"Oh, when you say yes, we always do that."

"That's right. You see, my word is so important to me that I never want to lie to you. If I tell you yes, I make every effort to be sure that thing happens. I want you to know that the truth is important. As your mom and as an example of how Christians ought to live, I want you to see that you can count on my word in the same way you can count on God's Word when He has said something to you."

Mark appreciated my yeses and my we'll-sees after that.

As our children become young adults, it may be necessary to speak uncomfortable truths to them when they are dishonoring God with their lifestyles, making poor financial choices, making poor relationship choices, etc. If we're dealing with moral issues that are precarious to one's faith, here's where speaking the truth in love comes in. We are responsible to share the truth of the Word with our wayward young adults. Again, we can still do this in love and preserve the relationship if our grown children do not initiate pulling themselves away.

When it comes to speaking the truth to our employees or people who volunteer to work with or for us, honesty with them is no less important than it would be with our children. Leviticus 19:11–12 says, "You shall not steal, nor deal falsely, nor lie to one another. And you shall not swear by My name falsely, nor shall you profane the name of your God: I am the Lord." When we tell the truth to those who work for us, we bring honor to the name of God. Eugene Peterson translates Colossians 4:1 in The Message Bible to say, "And masters, treat your servants considerately. Be fair with them. Don't forget for a minute that you, too, serve a Master—God in heaven"

(MSG). Even if it is a hard truth that has to be shared, you wouldn't want God lying to you, so don't lie to your employees.

Check Yourself

Do you have a hard truth that needs to be shared with an adult child or an employee? Write the problem down and place it in a basket. In your group, pull the problems from the basket and as a group discuss strategies for approaching and carrying out the necessary conversations.

Truth to Power

Are we speaking truth to power? Sometimes, it may seem most uncomfortable to speak the truth to our superiors. Lots of us are challenged to lie to keep ourselves out of trouble when we've made a mistake, but our lies are bound to find us out. Then the situation will be even worse. But we are not talking about telling our superiors the truth about something we've done. We're not talking about speaking *the* truth to someone in power, but speaking truth to power, telling someone in power about that person's mistake, misstep, misconception, or misinterpretation. This boss, teacher, department head, director, pastor, police officer, judge, or government official is not always right, and we may deem it appropriate to be the one to tell that to them. Lots of times, this is an impossibility without incurring negative repercussions upon oneself, so judge carefully. Does the issue really need to be discussed? Are you indeed the one to tell it? If so, when is the right time and how should you bring it up? Separate yourself from a superior who is trying to involve you in illegal activity and unwanted sexual advances. Stop such things immediately upon your first indication that it is happening. First Thessalonians 5:22 directs us to "abstain from all appearance of evil" (KJV). These are serious infractions and intrusions upon your life, so such activities must be stopped. God can provide you with another job if things are about to go too far.

We do have a biblical example of someone who had to speak truth to power. The *The Lexham Bible Dictionary* explains what happened when Nathan the prophet spoke truth to power in a situation with King David.

> Nathan's second oracle concerns David's adultery with Bathsheba and the ensuing murder of Bathsheba's husband, Uriah. In this episode (2 Sam 11–12), David breaks God's commandments and abuses his royal power. God disapproves and sends Nathan to confront David.
>
> Rather than accusing David outright, Nathan presents a parable about a rich man, a poor man, and the poor man's beloved ewe lamb (2 Sam 12:1–4). When David condemns the rich man for appropriating the poor man's lamb, Nathan shifts the focus to David's sin and delivers God's judgment against him for adultery and murder (2 Sam 12:5–12). Nathan's oracle

includes a three-part sentence: David's household will be rife with violence; another man will commit adultery against David in public; and Bathsheba's child will die (2 Sam 12:10–14). All three punishments happen just as Nathan predicts (2 Sam 12:15–18; 13:23–29; 16:20–23; 18:9–15).[2]

Definitely pray about what, how, and when to approach a person in power with an accusation, criticism, or discussion of an issue that shows him or her in a negative light. It may be best not to approach that person alone so that you will have a witness and some protection if the conversation goes sideways. Be wise in your dealings here.

Check Yourself

Are you in a situation where you need to speak truth to a person in power? Discuss this with your group and gather their opinions as to how you should go about approaching this person.

---

[2] McWhirter, J. (2016). Nathan the Prophet. In J. D. Barry, D. Bomar, D. R. Brown, R. Klippenstein, D. Mangum, C. Sinclair Wolcott, ... W. Widder (Eds.), *The Lexham Bible Dictionary*. Bellingham, WA: Lexham Press.

Truth to Self

Are we being honest with ourselves? Oh, we can lay it on other people thick and readily, but when it comes to speaking the truth to ourselves, we can easily fall short. One of Michael Jackson's songs speaks to this very point. The lyrics of "Man in the Mirror" discuss how the person is looking out at the world and seeing things he should care about. Then the chorus suggests that the person looks at himself, at the man in the mirror, and sees that only he can make the necessary changes in himself that need to be made to make him a better person.

James 1:22 –25 says, "But be doers of the word, and not hearers only, deceiving yourselves. For if anyone is a hearer of the word and not a doer, he is like a man observing his natural face in a mirror; for he observes himself, goes away, and immediately forgets what kind of man he was. But he who looks into the perfect law of liberty and continues in it and is not a forgetful hearer but a doer of the work, this one will be blessed in what he does."

So it's time to start speaking the truth to yourself about your past, your present, and your future. We lie to ourselves about the past when we don't go back and accept the hand life dealt us. There is absolutely nothing we can do to change the past. We had no say in our family of origin, our family's financial situation, or our living conditions. And now as we look back on the elementary, middle, and high schools we attended; the friends we did or didn't make, the university we did or didn't attend; the men we dated; the man we did or didn't marry; the jobs we did or didn't secure, the items we did or didn't buy, all the money we spent, the successes and the traumas—none of what happened before this moment can now be changed. All we can do is accept it, learn from it, and let God give us opportunities to share the wisdom we have learned.

If you are still alive, stop feeling guilty about your past mistakes. The money you wasted, the abortion, the neglect of someone you should have cared about—whatever is making you beat yourself up, since you can't change it, you have to move on. Every sin in forgivable except the sin of dying without knowing Christ. God died for every sin, even the worst sin you can think of. Stop letting your skeletons run your life. Skeletons have no muscle! I find that when I expose my skeletons, they don't even rattle anymore.

Believe it or not, we can also lie to ourselves about the present. The maxim "Know Thyself" has been attributed to many Greek philosophers and writers including Socrates and Plato. Also, in *Poor Richard's Almanac*, Benjamin Franklin states, "There are three things extremely hard, steel, a diamond, and to know one's self." And in Shakespeare's *Hamlet*, as Polonius is giving his son some pearls of wisdom, he connects the thought with telling the truth to others. Polonius tells his son Laertes, "This above all: to thine ownself be true, and it must follow, as the night the day, thou canst not then be false to any man" (Act 1, Scene 3).

Check Yourself

What are your strengths? What are your weaknesses? How are those weaknesses hindering your present?

How can you turn your weaknesses into strengths, to use them as stepping-stones rather than stumbling blocks?

Finally, did you know that we can lie to ourselves about our future? The one important truth about our future is that those of us who know Christ in the pardon of our sins are on our way to heaven. That reality should color the rest of our days on earth. As daughters of the King, we are above and not beneath, the head and not the tail, chosen of the Lord, a new creation, and the righteousness of God in Christ: and that's just for starters! God loves us, so everything about life is up. Since God is for us, nothing can win against us. Even the downs are tempered because we're held firmly and securely in His powerful hands.

R.I.S.E.

Radical change.

What is out of whack in my habits, thoughts, or actions that need to be radically changed? Are you always completely honest? What lies do you tell? Tell the truth about your past and your present. It's understandable if you decline to write your lies in this book; however, perhaps you trust your study group enough to share some things you have lied about, or some things you are currently lying about. The purpose of this sharing experience is to expose that which needs to be excised. As my pastor says, "You cannot fix what you will not face."

_____

_____

_____

Initiated by God.
What is Scripture telling me about this/these issue(s)?

_____

_____

_____

Submission to the Holy Spirit's direction.
How is the Holy Spirit directing me to carry out the necessary changes?

_____

_____

_____

Emergence into full understanding (and readiness to pass the information on).
Upon making the necessary lifestyle changes, in what ways am I being led to share my new understanding with those around me?

_____

_____

_____

Chapter Nine

Anger versus Anger without Sin

"Be angry, and do not sin": do not let the sun go down on your wrath, nor give place to the devil. Ephesians 4:26 –27

Psychologist and emotion researcher, Robert Plutchik, lists eight basic emotions: anger, fear, sadness, disgust, surprise, anticipation, trust, and joy. Any emotion that is not tempered or balanced will cause us trouble. According to the website *Live Bold and Bloom*[3], "[Plutchik] argued that each of these emotions triggers behavior with a high survival value, such as our fight or flight response to fear," and the fight or flight response exists because of the sudden release of adrenalin. Anger is an emotion that, like all those other emotions, must be brought under our control, meaning adrenalin release must be controlled. Too much anger, i.e. too much adrenalin, triggers problematic physical issues.

In Jacquelyn Cafasso's November 1, 2018 article on the Healthline Media website, she reviewed Dr. Debra Sullivan, PhD, MSN, RN, CNE, COI. The article says:

---

[3] https://liveboldandbloom.com/04/self-improvement/ultimate-list-emotions

Over time, persistent surges of adrenaline can damage your blood vessels, increase your blood pressure, and elevate your risk of heart attacks or stroke. It can also result in anxiety, weight gain, headaches, and insomnia. To help control adrenaline, you'll need to activate your parasympathetic nervous system, also known as the "rest-and-digest system." The rest-and-digest response is the opposite of the fight-or-flight response. It helps promote equilibrium in the body, and allows your body to rest and repair itself.[4]

Along with the problematic physical issues related to anger come problematic spiritual ones as well. Sin is our big spiritual problem. Listed in the Bible as ways to avoid sin are recognizing the fear of the Lord (Ex. 20:20), hiding God's Word in our heart (Ps. 119:11), and avoiding anger (Eph. 4:26). So, in our quest to be women God can bless, we must obey the point of the verse in question by avoiding sin related to the emotion of anger.

The Greek word parorgizo that is used here for "anger" is not used anywhere else in the Bible. The word means "to provoke to anger," however, some understand it to mean "to be provoked or irritated." The point being made in the context is still clear: whether we are the one making someone angry, or we are the one who has been provoked into being angry—provoker or provokee—either way, we are not supposed to let the

---

[4] https://www.healthline.com/health/adrenaline-rush

condition of anger linger from one day to the next. God is telling us to get over it.

Now, God does not usually tell us why He gives us His commands, but in this case, He does. He gives us two great reasons why we are to let the anger go. First, as already mentioned, holding on to anger can provoke us to commit sin. Sin separates us from Him and leads to death. Then second, holding on to anger gives the devil an opportunity to get involved in the situation. And when Satan becomes involved, the end result of actions driven by anger will be the opposite of what God's Word would have for our lives, and will distort the image of God in and through us. (In only one instance is anger ever productive, and that is when the anger is righteous indignation. We will take this up later in the chapter.)

We've all seen news stories that have chronicled the terrible outcome of anger. The big three negative emotions—hate, depression, and anger—drive a huge percentage of injuries and deaths through gun violence in the United States of America. Let me remind you of some of the heinous crimes that have been motivated by anger.

- The headline of the *Washington Post* September 26, 2011 article by Justin Jouvenal read, "Grandmother Killed Child out of Anger at Father, Prosecutor Says." The article went on to say:
  - Driven by "anger, hatred and revenge," a Fairfax County woman plotted to kill her 2-year-old granddaughter by tossing her off a 44-foot walkway at Tysons Corner Center

last November, Fairfax County's top prosecutor said in court Monday. Carmela Dela Rosa, 50, hatched the plan during a family outing as a way to get back at little Angelyn Ogdoc's father, James Ogdoc, prosecutors said. They said she blamed him for getting her daughter, Kathlyn Ogdoc, pregnant out of wedlock and splitting her from the family. (www.washingtonpost.com)

- A *New York Times* Associated Press article dated January 20, 2020 reported:
  - The suspected gunman opened fire after a near-collision between his older white sedan and the SUV around 9:30 p.m. The woman told police that the man cut in front of her SUV, forcing her to swerve as both vehicles sped north on a highway in northwest Dallas. The man then cut in front again, slamming on his brakes and nearly causing a crash. The woman said he then pulled up alongside the SUV and fired into the driver's side, according to police. The girl was shot once in her left side, police said. She was taken to a hospital and is in stable condition. (www.nytimes.com)

- On the subject of school shootings, CNN conducted its own study on data from 2009 through 2018. In a piece entitled, "10 Years, 180 School Shootings, 356 Victims" we read:

- We examined 10 years of shootings on K-12 campuses and found two sobering truths: School shootings are increasing, and no type of community is spared ... Over the past decade, there were at least 180 shootings at K-12 schools across the US. They happened in big cities and in small towns, at homecoming games and during art classes, as students are leaving campus in the afternoon and during late-night arguments in school parking lots. And they are happening more often. CNN analyzed locations, time of day, type of school and student demographics to better understand how this trauma grips the country. While school shootings disproportionately affect urban schools and people of color, mass shootings are more likely to occur at white, suburban schools ... "Today we have kids who are so isolated inside -- playing video games and glued to their (tablets) and everything else -- that they don't learn those problem-solving skills," says Mike Clumpner, a sworn police officer who specializes in active shooter training. "We continually see poor coping skills and poor conflict resolution skills," agrees former FBI agent Chris Cole, director of threat intervention services at the University of Wisconsin. "And as more of them (shootings) occur, it becomes sort of acceptable as 'that's a way I can settle my grievances.'" (www.cnn.com)

- The Federal Bureau of Investigation has quite a bit to say about hate crimes. Its website says:
    - Hate crimes are the highest priority of the FBI's Civil Rights program due to the devastating impact they have on families and communities. The Bureau investigates hundreds of these cases every year and works to detect and deter further incidents through law enforcement training, public outreach, and partnerships with community groups. Traditionally, FBI investigations of hate crimes were limited to crimes in which the perpetrators acted based on a bias against the victim's race, color, religion, or national origin. In addition, investigations were restricted to those wherein the victim was engaged in a federally protected activity. With the passage of the Matthew Shepard and James Byrd, Jr., Hate Crimes Prevention Act of 2009, the Bureau became authorized to also investigate crimes committed against those based on biases of actual or perceived sexual orientation, gender identity, disability, or gender.
    - In 2017, the most recent FBI statistic I found, a whopping 7,175 hate crimes were reported.

Clearly, anger is a problem in our culture, but as we all know, anger is not a new phenomenon. The earliest case of anger carried out to its ultimate, tragic conclusion is found in the first chapters of the Bible. Genesis chapter 4 records the account of Cain and Abel, the first sons of Adam and Eve. When the boys grew up, Cain became a farmer, and Abel became a shepherd. One day, the brothers decided to give God an offering. Cain offered fruit and Abel offered the firstborn of his flock. The Scriptures say, "And the Lord respected Abel and his offering, but He did not respect Cain and his offering. And Cain was very angry, and his countenance fell" (Genesis 4:4b –5 NKJV).

God saw Cain's attitude and asked him why he was angry and why he looked so mad. God went on to explain saying, " If you do well, will you not be accepted? And if you do not do well, sin lies at the door. And its desire *is* for you, but you should rule over it" (Genesis 4:7). The description of Cain's offering did not include any adjectives telling us that his fruit was the best or in any way sacrificial; however, Abel's offering included a blood sacrifice and was the first or the best of his flock. God may have continued to explain this distinction to Cain if Cain had humbly asked God what He meant by "if you do not do well." But Cain wasn't hearing what God had to say. At least, he wasn't letting what God had to say change his attitude. After this admonition from God, Cain allowed his anger to take over, so he went out and murdered his brother.

Anger spawned by jealousy is pretty common. We get mad because we either want what someone else has, or we sense that someone wants what we have. Cain wanted the recognition for his offering that Abel got for his, so Cain got mad. Someone else gets the promotion we know we are qualified to receive, so we get mad. Someone else's child is accepted into that exclusive school because that family knows the principal, not because that kid's grades are better than our kid's, so we get mad. Someone else gets engaged and it's not us again, so we get mad.

We women get mad if we see another woman fawning over our man and he seems to be enjoying it. We're ready to fight. We may lash out at the woman, (but we know that if there's another woman involved, she is really not our problem) but we'll most likely read our man the riot act. We know that men get jealous too thinking that some other man is trying to elbow his way into his woman's graces. In the Bible, Potiphar, Joseph's Egyptian employer, fell for the lie his wife told him, and threw Joseph in prison for flirting with his wife (see Genesis 39).

Interestingly enough, anger itself is not the problem. Our response to our anger is what's dangerous. Our anger may well be warranted. We may well have deserved the promotion, our child should have been accepted into that school, and it is hard being lonely while we keep getting invitations to everyone else's wedding. And indeed, our anger is hard to shake when it is kindled by the possibility of losing the one we love. In every case, God is still saying to us, "Be careful with this anger. Sin lies at the door and desires to rule over you."

Check Yourself

What gets your jealousy anger riled up? Is it jealousy related to your man, your children, your job, your possessions, your friendships, etc.? Honestly discuss these jealousies and come up with alternative ways to dispel the anger you feel in these situations.

We also get angry for other reasons besides jealousy. My anger button is injustice. This response to mistreatment is borne out early in life for most of us. If you've ever been around preschoolers for any amount of time, you've heard the words screamed or whined in anguish, "That's not fair!" You can say that I haven't outgrown this toddler angst if you'd like but check yourself in this area first. When you're lied on, overleapt for a promotion, misunderstood and then judged, misquoted and then accused, or mistreated and allowed no recourse, I'm pretty sure that's your that's-not-fair scream, whine, complaint, and suit I hear.

Once on my job, my anger was riled up over being misunderstood and left with no recourse. Someone had misread my intentions and instead of speaking directly to me, that person approached my supervisor intimating that my intention for my action was negative. My supervisor did not allow me to confront my accuser to explain my action and correct his or her wrong perception. I was just forced to make the change. My sense of injustice protested from within, "That's just not fair!" I was angry.

What did I do with my anger? There was nothing I could do but swallow it. Trust me, I had to strain to swallow it, but the sun went down, and there was no more conversation to be had with the supervisor. I sought counsel of two people I trusted, and although both agreed with me that the original person who lodged the complaint should have been told to come to me, I should let it go since that ship had sailed. The right option now was to turn my feelings over to God and just move on with my job. Many times, the right thing to do is the hard thing to do.

Now you may be thinking, *Sharon, get real. This little incident is nothing compared to what happened to me. I have a real reason to be angry.*

Perhaps your situation is more major. You could be angry how you were treated in court, your man's infidelity, a careless drunk driver who injured or killed your loved one, stolen money or property, an unforeseen illness, a job loss. It's not that God does not care about the reason for your anger. He is concerned about the formation of His Son's character in your life as you handle that anger. How is your handling of your anger a reflection of the life of Christ in you?

Check Yourself

What are your anger buttons? Injustice could very well be on your list. If you are alone, journal about your anger buttons. If you are with a group, discuss the last time those buttons were pushed. If you can't think of any anger buttons, and you are in a group of people who have known you for a while, ask them if they can identify any of your buttons for you. Also, let your group know if someone mentions a button you didn't think you had, but now that they mention it, you realize that button is one of yours too.

As mentioned earlier, the one instance in which anger is productive is when the anger is righteous indignation. In the collection *Pseudo-Clementine Literature*,[5] the explanation of righteous indignation is as follows…

> For this is righteous and necessary anger, by which every one is indignant with himself, and accuses himself for those things in which he has erred and done amiss; and by this indignation a certain fire is kindled in us, which, applied as it were to a barren field, consumes and burns up the roots of vile pleasure, and renders the soil of the heart more fertile for the good seed of the Word of God.[6]

---

[5] Roberts, A., Donaldson, J., & Coxe, A. C. (Eds.). (1886). Introductory Notice to Pseudo-Clementine Literature. In *Fathers of the Third and Fourth Centuries: The Twelve Patriarchs, Excerpts and Epistles, the Clementina, Apocrypha, Decretals, Memoirs of Edessa and Syriac Documents, Remains of the First Ages* (Vol. 8, p. 69). Buffalo, NY: Christian Literature Company.

[6] Pseudo-Clement of Rome. (1886). Recognitions of Clement. In A. Roberts, J. Donaldson, & A. C. Coxe (Eds.), M. B. Riddle (Trans.), *Fathers of the Third and Fourth Centuries: The Twelve Patriarchs, Excerpts and Epistles, the Clementina, Apocrypha, Decretals, Memoirs of Edessa and Syriac Documents, Remains*

We should be angry enough about our own sin that our anger lights a fire in us that will burn out everything in us that is not like God. The fire would then fertilize the soil of our hearts in such a way that the "good seed of the Word of God" will find nourishing pasture. What God wants for us will grow as plenteously as the sin used to cover the landscape of our lives.

Righteous indignation should also be kindled when God's reputation is at stake. We should have an issue with it when people disrespect Him. After all, jealousy for His own honor and glory is what pushes God's anger button. Now don't get it twisted like the famous talk show host did. She misunderstood the phrase "God is a jealous God" and declared that she didn't want the god of organized religion if he was jealous of her. God is not jealous of her, of you, of me, or of any person. He is jealous for His glory that He absolutely refuses to share. Since we are made in the image of God, we are wired the exact same way. When we work, we expect to get paid for the work we've done. We would be downright angry if we did the work but some other random person got the check we earned. In essence, we are jealous for the money due to us. God created the universe, keeps it from flying apart, and allows every breath we take, yet we attribute our blessings to everyone and everything else but God. God says, "I don't think so." All glory belongs to Him and, again, He refuses to share that paycheck with anyone or anything else.

---

of the First Ages (Vol. 8, p. 153). Buffalo, NY: Christian Literature Company.

Check Yourself

When have you gotten angry with righteous indignation— with anger about that which God would be angry about?

In order to understand righteous indignation a little better, in each of the following instances, journal or discuss with your group why God got angry and what He did about it.

- Genesis 6–8

So much evil in the world. Flooded the earth.

- Exodus 32:9–14

Stiff neck Israelites was going to destroyed but relented

- Mark 11:15–26

Jesus upset because of use of temple for gain. He threw tables over + stopped the merchandise

R.I.S.E.

Radical change. What is out of whack in your life in regard to your anger management? What are your anger buttons?

Initiated by God. What is Scripture telling me about anger?

- So then, my beloved brethren, let every man be swift to hear, slow to speak, slow to wrath; for the wrath of man does not produce the righteousness of God. James 1:19-20
- Stop being angry! Turn from your rage! Do not lose your temper—it only leads to harm. For the wicked will be destroyed, but those who trust in the Lord **will possess the land. Psalm 37:8-9 (NLT)**
- What is causing the quarrels and fights among you? Don't they come from the evil desires at war within you? You want what you don't have, so you scheme and kill to get it. You are jealous of what others have, but you can't get it, so you fight and wage war to take it away from them. Yet you don't have what you want because you don't ask God for it. James 4:1-2 (NLT)
- Sensible people control their temper; they earn respect by overlooking wrongs. Proverbs 19:11 (NLT)
- Do not be quickly provoked in your spirit, for anger resides in the lap of fools. Ecclesiastes 7:9
- A gentle answer deflects anger, but harsh words make tempers flare. Proverbs 15:1 (NLT)

- A hot-tempered person starts fights; a cool-tempered person stops them. Proverbs 15:18 (NLT)

Submission to the Holy Spirit's direction. How is the Holy Spirit directing me to carry out the necessary changes?

Emergence into full understanding (and readiness to pass the information on). Upon making the necessary lifestyle changes related to my anger, in what ways am I being led to share my new understanding with those around me?

Chapter Ten

Stealing versus Working

Let him who stole steal no longer, but rather let him labor, working with his hands what is good, that he may have something to give him who has need. Ephesians 4:28

Women whom God can bless do not steal; they work with their hands and earn what they have from their good works in order to be a blessing to others who are in need. That sentence should be obvious to everyone reading this book, so why isn't that the opening and the closing statement of this chapter with nothing in between? Well, because the truth is, God's women do steal and that's why we have arrived at this point in our discussion. If we truly desire to be women God can bless, we will need to retrain our brains to see stealing for what it really is and make a determination to cut it out.

Stealing We Excuse

<u>We Excuse Our Stealing of God's Tithes and Offerings</u>

Okay, don't close this book. Women God can bless are obedient to the whole counsel of Scripture, and God speaks to us directly about this subject of giving in church. In Malachi chapter 3, God communicates through the prophet that the Messiah is coming but the people of God have broken the covenant He had made with them. As God lays out the case against them, He asks the rhetorical question, "Will a man rob God?" He answers His own query, reading their minds in the process. "Yet you have robbed Me! But you say, 'In what way have we robbed You?' In tithes and offerings" (Malachi 3:8). The nation was cursed because they had neglected this practice. So clearly, women God can bless are women who participate in tithing and giving offerings.

Just as a refresher, what exactly is a tithe? By definition, the word "tithe" means "tenth." Our tithe is to be 10 percent of all of our increase. Our offerings are any amount of the 90 percent that we have left. God goes on in the Malachi passage to explain exactly how tithing works and how it benefits us:

> Bring all the tithes into the storehouse,
> That there may be food in My house,
> And try Me now in this,"
> Says the Lord of hosts,
> "If I will not open for you the windows of heaven
> And pour out for you such blessing
> That there will not be room enough to receive it.
>
> "And I will rebuke the devourer for your sakes,
> So that he will not destroy the fruit of your ground,

Nor shall the vine fail to bear fruit for you in the field,"
Says the Lord of hosts;
"And all nations will call you blessed,
For you will be a delightful land,"
Says the Lord of hosts. (Malachi 3:10- 12)

Tithes and offerings are the financial income plan for the church. The people of God are to bring their tithes and offerings to the house of God to supply for its needs. The church should have outreach ministries such as feeding and clothing the poor, visiting the sick and incarcerated, helping those in precarious financial straits, and reaching the world with the gospel. In addition to being a spiritual body the church also has physical needs. Leaders like pastors and office workers need to be paid physical money, not just our thanks. Our church buildings need to have electricity, running water, and building maintenance. Sometimes, God has blessed us with structures that need many other things too like heat during the winter months, air conditioning during the summer, and even telephone service. The power, water, and phone companies do not give their utilities to us for free.

To meet the needs of our local church body, we are to give God 10 percent of our income. Just like God didn't want the sickly animals from the flock as an offering, He requires the best we have to give of our income. That tithe check should be written first; in other words, the money we give God ought to come off the top, not as an afterthought from whatever we have left over after we have paid everyone else. "Honor the Lord with your possessions, and with the first fruits of all your increase; so your barns will be filled with plenty, and your vats will overflow with new wine" (Proverbs 3:9-11).

Here's what we often forget. We are not the only ones giving. God has promised to give back to us when we tithe and give offerings. Read the Malachi and Proverbs passages above again. Look at what God has promised:

- Heaven's open windows pouring down a blessing so vast we won't have room to receive it all
- The devourer's power thwarted so that what we have will not be destroyed
- People around us will proclaim that we are indeed blessed.
- Our "barns" will be full of plenty; we will have an abundance of what we need.
- Our "vats" will overflow with new wine; fresh blessings will keep coming.

I knew about tithing because I grew up in church as a PK (pastor's kid); however, at one particularly distressful time in my life, I had neglected the practice. I was teaching in a Christian high school and was responsible for instructing some of the religion classes. In preparing the curriculum, I had designed for our seniors to study the minor prophets. Of course, we had to cover the book of Malachi, so we had to study this passage on tithing. While teaching my students, I had to admit to them that I wasn't currently tithing, but God's Word says

I should, so I was going to start. I challenged them to do the same.

After some discussion to break through the excuses, most of the students said they'd try it. I told them that we would stick with it until God's promises stopped working on our behalf. If any of my students stopped tithing, it wasn't because God failed to meet their needs, and I have never stopped again. Several lyrical lines of an old church spiritual say, "You can't beat God giving, no matter how you try. The more you give, the more He gives to you."

It has been said that tithing is the debt we owe; offerings are the seed we sow. Due to God's radical financial plan related to tithing and giving offerings, I have become a radical tither. As long as I gave God His tithe first, He always made sure every one of my needs was met. He did it through things like unexpected checks in the mail, mystery gifts of groceries showing up on my porch, finding money on the ground, invitations to speak or preach, writing contracts, new business ideas, and a new husband who took over the paying of household bills. He also blessed my children and me with good health so I could avoid medical bills; a decent running car so I could avoid large repair bills; and appliances that kept operating so I could avoid needing to fix or replace them.

When we don't tithe, money runs through our fingers like sand. The money we refused to give to God we end up losing due to breakdowns, illnesses, missed opportunities, and stolen ideas. Whether I earn, find, or am gifted money, I tithe off of every dime that comes into my possession. I intend to be a woman ready to receive the windows-of-heaven blessing from our Father God.

So let's debunk some of the excuses I've heard for not tithing.

- "There are enough people giving money in church. Nobody will miss the little amount I could give. Besides, my church is doing fine. It doesn't need my money."

Hopefully, there are enough people giving money in your church to take care of its needs; however, what does that have to do with you? You are not told to give your tithes and offerings only if your church tells you there's a particular need. God says that by not paying your tithes and offerings, you are robbing Him, picking His pocket, and keeping His hand away while He is trying to bless you.

- "This is an Old Testament injunction. It doesn't apply to us today, especially since we now have the New Testament."

Someone once said, "The Old Testament is the New Testament concealed; the New Testament is the Old Testament revealed." You don't get to pick and choose which parts of the Bible you like and which you don't. Only those passages that have been specifically changed by Scripture are up for exclusion. For example, we no longer obey the laws pertaining to the sacrificial system of the Old Testament temple because Jesus became the last sacrifice for sin that was necessary. (See Hebrews 7:26-27)

- "I'm not going to give the pastor all of my money."

Unless you are on the church's finance committee, you are not running the budget of the church. First of all, you misunderstand what happens with the monies taken up in the offerings. The pastor receives a salary; the rest of the monies go to cover the spiritual and business needs of the local body.

- "I can't afford to tithe."

From what we've just learned about tithing, you can't afford *not* to tithe. We don't give because God will bless us; we give because God said so. God's blessings are simply a fact that follows.

Check Yourself

Figure out your tithe. Write down the amount of money on your paycheck. Move the decimal one place to the left. That's the amount you owe to God as your tithe. For example, if your check is for $1,237.85, moving the decimal point one place to the left gives you $123.78. I would round up to $124.00 even. That should be the amount of your tithe and would leave you with $1,113.85 to take care of your personal business. You can give any amount from this to the Lord as an offering.

Now plan your offerings. For last year and this year, I decided to give a dollar in every offering in a church service when it's not the collection in which I have given my tithe. If I don't have a dollar, I will give some or all of the change I have in my wallet. Your offering plan can be anything you decide. Another example of planning your offering could be what I used to do with my children when they were young. We had three piles: Tithe, Save, and Bless Others. I would allow them to see me writing out the tithe check. Then we would put away another 10 percent into our own savings account. Finally, we would put away a regular, agreed-upon amount in our "Bless Others" account. That was our offering. The offering account could go to someone in need in our church that week, or the "Bless Others" account might grow over several months before we heard of someone in our congregation who needed that much money.

We Excuse Our Stealing in Regard to Taxes

Jesus was always under attack by the religious leaders of His day. The chief priests, scribes, and elders (the CP's, S's and E's) of the Jerusalem synagogue were especially perturbed by Him because they couldn't stop or block the influence He had over the people. One day, these leaders decided to trap Jesus by getting Him to speak disrespectfully against Rome. That would have been suicide! So, these leaders employed other leaders, the Pharisees and the Herodians (the P's and H's), to participate in their little scheme (see Mark 11 and 12).

Stealing versus Working

So, the P's and H's approached Jesus about whether or not good, law-abiding Jews ought to pay taxes. If Jesus said no and spoke against Rome, they could legitimately turn Him in as a dissident and get Roman law to convict Him. If He said yes, Jesus would be seen as a sympathizer with the Jews' archenemy. They could get the people to turn away from Him because they all hated the Roman rule under which they had to live.

Of course, Jesus was slicker than the slickest trick anyone could try to play on Him. He responded, "Whose is this image and superscription?"

And they said unto him, "Caesar's."

So, Jesus answered, "Render to Caesar the things that are Caesar's, and to God the things that are God's. (Mark 12:16-17)

All they could do was marvel at His ultimate cool!

Christians ought to pay their taxes and not steal from the government. In the United States, the Internal Revenue Service (IRS) makes sure we pay our fair share in federal and state taxes. Federal taxes pay for things like our country's officials (the president, senators, congressmen, etc.), our armed forces, government grants, national parks, and interstate highways. State and city taxes fund things like our governors' paychecks, fire departments, streetlights, libraries, the highway patrol, the police and state troopers, and street maintenance. We all enjoy the conveniences afforded us by the comforts our taxes pay for, so we should all pitch in.

Now we are not getting into the debate here as to whether or not you feel the tax laws are fair—that's another debate for another book. In general, though, if we're honest, we are not usually trying to withhold our taxes because of some noble, progressive, or altruistic reason. We just want more money in our pockets. The IRS may move slowly, but it will catch up to us and eventually take more from our checks than just the normal deductions because, as the last ditch effort to collect, our wages could be garnished to forcefully make us pay our share into the system. As we learned in the previous section of this chapter, we will have all the money we need and then some in our pockets if we give our tithes and offerings as we should. It is not necessary to defraud the government to have what we need. The one way to pay less taxes is to make less money. Do we want that? I don't think so.

Women of God are not only stealing from the government in the area of taxes, but we can also be guilty of stealing when we take unfair advantage of government programs. For example, both of our cars have handicapped license plates because my husband's conditions qualify him for the program. At any given time, he could be driving either car and would be in need of using the handicapped parking spaces. However, the law says that I cannot park in a handicapped space unless he is in the car with me, so I am literally stealing the space (I am also lying) if I park in a handicapped spot for the sake of convenience when I am shopping by myself. Stop doing it. One of my friends actually got caught using her husband's handicapped placard without him in the car. She was fined $1,000.00. Not having that kind of money, she begged the judge to allow her to do community service instead, so he ordered her to do thirty-five hours of service. All for saving a few steps. Not worth it.

Here in my state, the California Department of Public Health runs the WIC (Women, Infants, and Children) program. The program basically helps families get healthy food. I once overheard a conversation about gainfully employed parents benefitting from the program by lying about their income in order to get free milk for their kids. So, in reality, as a California taxpayer, this family was stealing from me. My tax money was buying the milk for them when their income adequately could have covered that expense.

Gaming the system is not okay. This family was saying, "So what? God has blessed us with good jobs and corresponding great paychecks, but God has still shortchanged us. His provision is not adequate to cover our daily needs. We can't trust God. We have to steal from others to get milk for our kids." Women whom God can bless depend on Him and do not need to be conniving in order to make ends meet.

Check Yourself

Are you gaming a government system for your own ends? Besides cheating the IRS, using handicapped placards illegitimately, or tricking the WIC system, are you guilty of being dishonest with any other government program or official? Admit it. Confess it. Stop it.

We Excuse Our Stealing in Regard to Copyright-Protected Items

When it comes to copyright law, many Christians don't stop to think about how we participate in stealing in this area. I'm sensitive to it because I'm an author and songwriter. When we make copies of large tracts of a book, we are stealing income from the author. Whoever received those copies should have bought the book, thereby giving the author payment for his or her her copyrighted material. When we copy music, we are stealing from the composers and artists because the copy means I didn't have to buy the music. We are also breaking copyright laws when our choir performs copyrighted music in a church concert, we record it, and sell the CDs. That music cannot be used for resale nor used to back a performance (like a dance) in any fund-raising program without permission.

Most of us know that buying bootleg CD s of movies is stealing as well. Now with the different movie stations that are easily accessible on our television sets, this temptation is possibly going to go away. However, since there still could be some rogue movie CD sellers out there, this warning bears mentioning.

Put yourself in the position of the composer, original performer, or author. If that music or book earns income for the writer, we are stealing to use it without permission. Thou shalt not steal (Exodus 20:15).

Check Yourself

What copyrighted material do you have that you did not buy? Do you think you are sending a good message by continuing to own these items? What should you do about this? What will you do about it?

<u>We Excuse Our Stealing of Items and Time from Work</u>

This point can be seen as fitting under the category covered by the verse "render unto Caesar the things which are Caesar's." We owe our employer exactly what our contract says we owe. Except for taking the breaks mandated by the law, if we are hired to work a forty-hour week, that's how many hours we should work. We are stealing when we use our employer's time to goof off or take care of our personal business.

We are also stealing if we take items meant for use at work. How many of us have pens, pencils, sticky note pads, and markers in our possession at home that are meant to be used at the company for company business? And the ink, toner, and paper are also to be used for the company's purposes, not to make flyers for the church Annual Day or your sister's baby shower.

Check Yourself

How much of your employer's time do you use for yourself? In other words, if you were paid for the actual number of hours you worked for your employer, how much would your paycheck really be? Look around your home and in your purse right now. Do you have anything in your possession for your personal use that was bought by your employer to be used on the job?

We Excuse Our Stealing of Others' Ideas

We communicate with one another in a vast variety of ways these days. In the old days, we could talk in person, on the telephone, by writing letters, or by sending telegrams. Now, we can still talk in person, on the phone, and through letters, but telegrams are no longer necessary because we have the internet. And via the World Wide Web, we can communicate in so many ways it's crazy. We can touch the lives of people around the world all at once.

The thing is, people we don't even know can be out there listening in on our ideas. What's to stop them from claiming those ideas as their own and then capitalizing on them? And what's to stop us from doing the same thing?

Ideas cannot be copyrighted until they are put in some kind of fixed format. So, if you have an idea for a product, you may need a patent; for a book, you will need to write it down. Once your book is published, your publisher will secure the official copyright for you. If you self-publish your book, it's not hard to secure the copyright for yourself. If God has given you a great idea for anything that may become a source of income for you, work it up to a proposal stage and protect it until you get it to a stage that is able to have copyright protection. (I would not recommend that you prospective authors spend money on securing copyright protection if few people are interested in what you are writing.)

We are not the only people in the universe with the same idea. For example, lots of ladies are starting conferences to encourage other women; it's likely that no one stole your women's conference idea unless you outlined it for the women who are now enjoying the time away. In several instances, I feel people used my ideas to start their own quests and then chose not to include me. That is hurtful and disappointing when those women are Christians and I counted them as friends. Live and learn. God has continued to give me new ideas and refinements of the old ideas that have since grown into profitable ventures for me. When you are one of God's anointed daughters, you are a woman God can and will bless in the presence of your enemies.

We need to be honest and careful not to capitalize on one another's ideas. Following "don't steal" and "don't lie" comes a related commandment which says, "You shall not covet your neighbor's house; you shall not covet your neighbor's wife, nor his male servant, nor his female servant, nor his ox, nor his donkey, nor anything that *is* your neighbor's" (Exodus 20:17). The last phrase, "nor anything that is your neighbor's" includes ideas. If you hear something great from a friend, you can let her know that you've conceptualized ways to expand on her great thoughts. Tell her that you think her idea would be a great business, and then ask her if she'd like to explore the expansion of that idea with you. If not, ask her if she wouldn't mind if you ran with it on your own. Keep everything on the up-and-up.

Check Yourself

Have you purposely or inadvertently stolen an idea that has become financially profitable for you? What do you think is the right thing for you to do about that now?

Has someone stolen one of your ideas and become financially rewarded? Unless you can prove it, there is nothing you can do about this but forgive them and move on. Be more careful next time when it comes to talking about your idea. Pray for God to give you direction toward those you can trust.

We Excuse Our Stealing of Time from God

Finally, as we wrap up our discussion on stealing, let's talk about how we steal time from God. After all He's done and all He continues to do for us every single day, we can really be stingy with the amount of time we spend with Him. Just before He ascended to heaven after His resurrection, Jesus' last admonition to His disciples, and by extension to us, involved our time. He instructed, "Go therefore and make disciples of all the nations, baptizing them in the name of the Father and of the Son and of the Holy Spirit, teaching them to observe all things that I have commanded you …" (Matthew 28:19 –20a). Going, baptizing, and teaching are verbs, action words, indicating activities that will take time for us to perform.

We are to be working in the Lord's vineyard, using our gifts for His purposes. Ephesians 2:10 tells us that "we are His workmanship, created in Christ Jesus for good works, which God prepared beforehand that we should walk in them." And Hebrews 6:10 says that "God is not unjust so as to forget your work and the love which you have shown toward His name, in having ministered and in still ministering to the saints" (NAS).

Are you an active member of your local church? But more than just attending services and Bible study, are you involved in different auxiliaries like the prayer team, outreach committee, prison visit group, choir, usher board, Sunday school teachers, or the group who visits the sick?

Check Yourself

God gives every one of us the same amount of time each week—168 hours—to get things done. Make yourself a chart with seven columns across the top for the days of the week and twenty-four rows to represent every hour of the day and night. Now fill it in to give yourself a picture of how you spend your time. Here's how to fill out your chart. In blue, cross out the hours when you are…

1. … asleep
2. … traveling to and from work (or whatever you have to do)
3. … at work
4. … cooking and eating
5. … caring for children
6. … involved in self-care (bathroom time, dressing, exercising, salon, nail shop, etc.)
7. … attending classes (school)

Now using red (to represent the blood of Jesus), cross out the hours when you are …

1. … attending church services
2. … attending Bible study
3. … reading your Bible in your own structured quiet time
4. … praying in your own structured quiet time
5. … participating in the work of any auxiliary apart from times during the church service (i.e., choir practice, visiting the prison or hospital, ministry meetings, etc.)
6. …participating in a ministry not related to your church

Now evaluate.

- How many hours are blue? Those are hours you spend on your personal life and pursuits. Figure out the percentage of your time that you spend involved in these activities. Divide the number of hours spent by 168. For example, if you spend forty hours a week at work, you spend almost 24 percent of your time at work. If you spend two hours in church and do no more faith-related activities, you spend only .01 percent of your time with God.
- How many hours are red? Those are the hours you spend on God's pursuits; hours representing activities you participate in because you are

a Christian. What percentage of your week do you spend on God's business?
- How many hours are blank? Those are the hours that represent your free time. What do you do during these hours? How much of that time is spent with loved ones, just resting, playing video games, watching TV, quietly thinking, etc.?
- We need rest. In fact, we are supposed to take a whole day every week as a sabbath. I definitely need to work on keeping this commandment. I bet you do too!

R.I.S.E.

Radical change. What is out of whack in my habits, thoughts, or actions related to stealing that needs to be radically changed?

Initiated by God. What is Scripture telling me about stealing?

Submission to the Holy Spirit's direction. How is the Holy Spirit directing me to carry out changes in the way I think about stealing?

Emergence into full understanding (and readiness to pass the information on). Upon making the necessary lifestyle changes, in what ways am I being led to share my new understanding about stealing with those around me?

Chapter Eleven

Wrath versus Being Kind

Let all ... wrath ... clamor, and evil speaking be put away from you, with all malice. And be kind to one another ... forgiving one another, even as God in Christ forgave you. Ephesians 4:31 –32

Wrath, *orgen* in Greek, means desire or violent passion, justifiable abhorrence, and punishment. In other words, wrath is the next step after anger. Wrath is the action that follows anger. You see, I can be angry and never do anything about it. However, if I allow anger to fester, wrath is born, and it causes me to act against its target.

If you refer back to chapter 9 of this book, the chapter about anger, you will remember our discussion of righteous indignation. That chapter says that "righteous indignation should... be kindled when God's reputation is at stake." The wrath of God is the result of God's righteous indignation. Romans 1:18 and 25 say that "the wrath of God is revealed from heaven against all ungodliness and unrighteousness of men, who suppress the truth in unrighteousness [and have] exchanged the truth of God for the lie and worshiped and served the creature rather than the Creator." That passage in Romans chapter 1 goes on to explain to us how God's wrath worked itself out as He gave those people over to the punishment their own sins created for them.

But as we also stated in chapter 9, rarely can we define our anger as righteous indignation. We get angry for a variety of reasons and then let our anger drive our thoughts toward wrath. We start planning what we are going to do to get that person back for making us angry. If we are going to be women God can bless, we are clearly told to "Let all … wrath … clamor, and evil speaking be put away … and be kind." Even more pointedly, Romans 12:19– 21 instructs us in this way:

> Beloved, do not avenge yourselves, but *rather* give place to [God's] wrath; for it is written, "Vengeance *is* Mine, I will repay," says the Lord. Therefore "If your enemy is hungry, feed him; if he is thirsty, give him a drink; for in so doing you will heap coals of fire on his head." Do not be overcome by evil but overcome evil with good (NKJV).

In other words, when we get angry because someone has done us wrong, Christians are to allow God to do the punishing. Instead of giving in to the temptation to "get them back," we are supposed to act in the totally opposite way. We're to feed our enemies and give them water if they're thirsty. God says that if we do this, our kind responsive actions will turn the situation around. Our job is to overcome evil with good; vengeance is His job. We are to be kind *(chrestoi* in Greek); that is, useful, gentle, and pleasant. We can trust Him to have our backs against our enemies. The punishment we could think up for our enemies is nothing compared to what God can do to take care of the situation.

Obviously, there are as many different reasons for wrath as there are individual situations in the world; however, we are going to focus on only two that I believe will bear out some major truths we need to take with us as women God can bless. We will discuss divorce and racial/gender prejudice.

Divorce

Unfortunately, one of the most common experiences many women share is the break-up of a romantic relationship, a divorce. Since God designed marriage to be a lifelong connection in which two people become one, He hates divorce. Malachi 2:16 says, "'For I hate divorce!' says the LORD, the God of Israel. 'To divorce your wife is to overwhelm her with cruelty,' says the LORD of Heaven's Armies. 'So guard your heart; do not be unfaithful to your wife'" (NLT).

We see why God hates divorce because of all the devastation it leaves in its wake. The Malachi verse above speaks to the husband's fault in the divorce. In the culture surrounding the writing of this verse, only men were allowed to legally end a marriage. It was the man's responsibility to care for his wife and provide a life for her. For a man to divorce his wife was to "overwhelm her with cruelty." A divorced woman in those times would most probably become an outcast, end up homeless, and see her life completely devastated.

God still holds husbands responsible for the success or demise of their marriages; however, we realize that wives also play their part in divorces. Women can be the ones who commit adultery or abandon the family (the two reasons why God allows divorce); however, our discussion is not about who is at fault. Our discussion here is about what we are supposed to do with the wrathful plans we make because of the hurt and anger we feel as a result of the divorce.

Over the years, Irene* watched her husband change. After starting out as young adults who met while working in the church's mission department, they married, completed their family with a little boy and a little girl, and bought a beautiful home. They were living the dream as Keith* worked for a nonprofit that he loved, and Irene enjoyed raising the kids and making their house a home.

But as mentioned, Irene watched Keith change. He became distant and violent, emotionally abusing her with name-calling and cursing, even often threatening to hit her. Irene prayed for God to bring back their early love, but things just got worse and worse. When the money for bills began to disappear, she really got worried. Creditors began to send threatening letters because bills and then the mortgage fell behind. She discovered he had left his job and had just been masquerading about going to work each day. Keith stopped attending church. Their son and daughter started exhibiting signs of fear and regression at school because of all the tension in the home. Keith even started pawning items (like his wedding ring) to get money for himself. After filing for bankruptcy, they lost their beautiful home and had to move into an apartment complex supplied to them by members of their church. Irene went back to work.

Through a series of events, Irene finally discovered that an affair and a gambling addiction were the causes of Keith's transformation. When confronted by their pastor, Keith refused to confess or repent and they ended up in divorce court.

Irene was angry. Her dreams about her marriage and her future had not included any of this madness. However, Irene made a decision that she would not lash out to carry out wrathful plans of retribution. She had trusted God all along the way and refused to blame God for the turn of events in her life. She determined not to talk disparagingly about Keith to their children. She turned him and his problems over to God.

Years passed in Irene's Irene's and Keith's stories. God continued to bless Irene and her children. She remarried an amazing man who took her children in as his own. Both kids graduated from college and are a benefit to everyone their lives touch. She is a homemaker again, living her dream as founder and CEO of her own entrepreneurial venture.

As for Keith, he has a strained relationship with the children at best. Irene didn't have to tell them of his shortcomings because he lived them out in front of them. He spent many years jumping from one dead-end job to another, lived on the street for a while, and is now suffering with some long-term physical health challenges. This looks like God's vengeance repaying Keith's treatment of Irene.

If you have been in or are going through a divorce, be careful to keep God in the midst of this horrific situation. Ask God how He wants you to proceed and then submit to His directions. If at all possible, disagree with your husband without being disagreeable. Don't let your lawyer determine how far you go at gouging your spouse. Your lawyer works for you, not the other way around. Yes, you should be awarded what's fair, but allow God to execute wrath. Until you can speak kindly with your husband, communicate through a friend or through your lawyer. Do not let your buttons be pushed as you seek to obey God's directive to be kind—useful, gentle, and pleasant—and overcome evil with good.

Check Yourself

1. Since God hates divorce, is there any way you and your husband can be reconciled?

   _____
   _____

2. How much of your divorce decree is a result of your wrath?

   _____
   _____

3. In what ways can you respond in kindness the next time you have to carry out an action or answer a communique regarding your divorce?

_____

_____

Racial Prejudice:

Prejudicial feelings can lead to wrath if we're not careful. In other words, when we feel hatred because we are prejudiced against someone, sometimes we think about how we can make those people suffer when who they are and how they look have nothing to do with the situation. Like other sins, racial prejudice goes back at least as far as the Bible.

Moses married a woman he met when he ran away from Egypt after the murder he committed was discovered. Miriam and Aaron, Moses' sister and brother, were none too happy with the wife he chose. Numbers 12:1-10 detail the situation:

> Then Miriam and Aaron spoke against Moses because of the Ethiopian woman whom he had married; for he had married an Ethiopian woman. So they said, "Has the LORD indeed spoken only through Moses? Has He not spoken through us also?" And the LORD heard it. (Now the man Moses was very humble, more than all men who were on the face of the earth.)

Suddenly the Lord said to Moses, Aaron, and Miriam, "Come out, you three, to the tabernacle of meeting!" So the three came out. Then the Lord came down in the pillar of cloud and stood in the door of the tabernacle, and called Aaron and Miriam. And they both went forward. Then He said,

"Hear now My words:
If there is a prophet among you,
I, the Lord, make Myself known to him in a vision;
I speak to him in a dream.
Not so with My servant Moses;
He is faithful in all My house.
I speak with him face to face,
Even plainly, and not in dark sayings;
And he sees the form of the Lord.
Why then were you not afraid
To speak against My servant Moses?"

So the anger of the Lord was aroused against them, and He departed. And when the cloud departed from above the tabernacle, suddenly Miriam became leprous, as white as snow. Then Aaron turned toward Miriam, and there she was, a leper.

Notice how Miriam and Aaron tried to disguise the real problem they were having with their brother Moses. The passage clearly says that they were speaking against Moses "because of the Ethiopian woman whom he had married." Yet they used their complaint about him getting all the spiritual attention as a cover-up for the real problem they had with Moses. This tells me that prejudice could very well be the underlying, real reason for the barriers people construct to keep them separated from people of a different race or culture.

God never intended for us to operate in a prejudicial manner. For example, the Bible is clear that God is okay with interracial marriage. As we read above, Moses married Zipporah, an Ethiopian woman. Rahab, the harlot of Jericho, married one of the men of Israel. Ruth, a Moabitess, married Boaz and became the great-grandmother of King David. And both Ruth and Rahab are in the direct line that led to Jesus Christ. If God had had a problem with interracial marriage, He never would have allowed history to turn in such a way as to include them in the family line of the Savior of the world.

As Christians, we have no business at all to hold prejudicial feelings and opinions against anyone of a different race from ourselves. The Bible uses phrases like "we are all one in Christ," "for all have sinned," "whosoever calls upon the name of the Lord shall be saved," and "God loved the world" in order to make the point that everyone stands equal— every person of every race— before Him.

We cannot allow our prejudices to color our reactions to others either. That's where wrath comes in. Our prejudices make us reach out to hurt people of other races. North America has an ugly history in regard to how people of color have always been treated. From the taking of Native American lands, to slavery, to Jim Crow, to red-lining, to legalized abortion (originally meant to be a genocidal tool), the United States of America has promoted racial inequality. These horrible actions perpetrated by one race of people upon another are proof of how far wrath will go.

Simple acts of kindness will counteract prejudicial wrath. Kindness begins in the heart and mind. If we are all equal in God's sight, we ought to be equal in each other's sight. If we are thinking any other way, we are in sin, and we need to repent and change our outlook about people of different races than our own.

Gender Prejudice:

Gender prejudice can be understood in two ways: prejudice toward a gender because of past hurts, and prejudice toward people who are not identifying with the gender they were assigned at birth. In the first case, for example, a woman can show gender prejudice toward men because men have hurt her throughout her life. She is not a lesbian because she is not attracted sexually to other women. She just hates men because of her previous negative history with them. When gender prejudice exists because of past wounds, no one has much of a problem with this. We may think that the person who has been hurt is taking things too far, but we tend to excuse and understand why they feel the way they feel, and we don't bother them about changing.

However, we Christians have a huge problem with gender prejudice when it comes to the homosexual question. In short, since the Bible lists homosexuality as a sin in several passages, many people who identify themselves as believers feel justified in shunning people who have identified themselves as SSA (same sex-attracted). The sad thing is that the same volatility is not perpetrated upon people bound by the other sins in the lists that include homosexuality. For example, 1 Corinthians 6:9-10 says, "Do you not know that the unrighteous will not inherit the kingdom of God? Do not be deceived. Neither fornicators, nor idolaters, nor adulterers, nor homosexuals, nor sodomites, nor thieves, nor covetous, nor drunkards, nor revilers, nor extortioners will inherit the kingdom of God." Fornicators, idolaters, adulterers, thieves, covetous people, and alcoholics are in the list, but are not treated in society the same as homosexuals. Many times, homosexuals receive the wrath of the congregation, while alcoholics are cheerfully welcomed to the AA meetings held in the church's multi-purpose room.

What's the point? Am I saying that alcoholics and thieves should start receiving the same wrath-induced attacks homosexuals now receive? No. Am I saying that alcoholism and thievery and homosexuality are okay in God's sight? No. I'm saying that the kindness we show to folks in the AA meeting should be extended to the fornicators, the covetous, and the homosexual community. People who are alcoholics, fornicators, thieves, or homosexuals cannot be hated because they fit into one of these categories. The point is, no matter what the sin is, every person must be reached out to with the compelling gospel message of salvation through Jesus Christ. Then, as people grapple with the Bible, God is perfectly able to draw any and every one to Himself. In Jesus' day, once people came to Him, He never compelled them to stay. His word was enough to keep them close to Him. We must stop letting gender prejudice keep us from befriending SSA folks. The opposite of wrath is kindness. Women God will bless are those who allow our genuine kindness to draw all people in. We can then love them up close while God takes care of communicating to them, like He continues to communicate to each of us the changes He wants to see.

Check Yourself

1. Are you prejudiced against people of any particular race? In what ways does your wrath show when it is targeted against someone of another race? Could you have a friendly meal with someone of another race?
2. Are you gender-prejudiced? In what ways do your comments about homosexual people show how you truly feel about them? Are your feelings and actions toward homosexual people the same as Jesus's feelings toward them? Could you have a friendly meal with someone who was SSA ?
3. How can you show kindness toward someone of a different race?
4. How can you show kindness toward a SSA individual?

R.I.S.E.

Radical change. What is out of whack in my habits, thoughts, or actions that needs to be radically changed in regard to divorce and prejudice?

Initiated by God. What is Scripture telling me about:

    a. My divorce?
    b. My prejudices?

Submission to the Holy Spirit's direction. How is the Holy Spirit directing me to carry out the necessary changes in the areas of:

    a. My divorce
    b. My prejudices

Emergence into full understanding (and readiness to pass the information on). Upon making the necessary lifestyle changes, in what ways am I being led to share my new understanding about divorce and about prejudices with those around me?

Chapter Twelve

Bitterness versus Being Tenderhearted and Forgiving

Let all bitterness ... be put away from you, with all malice. And be ... tenderhearted, forgiving one another, even as God in Christ forgave you. Ephesians 4:31-32

As we end our discussion about living as women God can bless, we will explore the destroyer known as bitterness. Why do I call it "the destroyer?" Bitterness is the destroyer because it attacks us from the inside. Just as wrath seeks to exact punishment on the one with whom we are angry, bitterness unleashes its venom into our spiritual bloodstream and poisons us from within.

Bitterness is the Greek word *pikria* and means "harshness and acridity." Something that is acrid is extremely sharp and stinging; it is something that is irritating to the eyes and nose. If we were caught in a fire and trapped long enough to be forced to start breathing in the smoke, our eyes would begin to sting, and we would start coughing and suffocating because of the acridity of the smoke. Bitterness is the smoke of the fire of anger. It occludes our vision, disabling our ability to detect anything clearly related to the anger-causing situation. Our anger simply becomes a slow burn within. And unless we can extricate ourselves, the longer the anger burns, the more damage it causes; alas, bitterness has taken root.

We readily recognize bitter people. Upon the mention of the situations that have caused their bitterness, they either become silent or launch into an uninterruptable tirade about that unfair treatment, that divorce, the court ruling, that demotion, etc. Everything looks and sounds to them like a conspiracy has been hatched against them. Eventually, they no longer smile.

Do you remember back in chapter 9 when I shared the situation I faced on my job when I felt I was treated unfairly? I thought I had swallowed my anger and moved on until I started writing this part of this chapter. Every time I thought about the situation, it burned on the inside that the complainer and my supervisor had won at the expense of an action of mine they refused to understand. I had not really turned that anger over to God. I realized that the only thing that would make it completely right for me would be if my explanation of my intention was accepted and I was allowed to go back to my action. As time moved along, the days and weeks did not serve to separate me from the incident. The sting of unfair treatment did not lessen. In fact, the injury had become a slow burn that only intensified whenever I thought about the incident or had to interface with my supervisor. Every comment to me, every look my way, was colored by an underlying cynicism.

I cannot be myself because being myself is frowned upon. All the other employees can be themselves, so I cannot be like everybody else; therefore, I'm not accepted on equal footing. If I cannot be myself, I cannot do my job efficiently and effectively. Perhaps this is all a part of a conspiracy to drum me out. I had better watch my back.

Without even realizing it until just now, at the writing of this chapter, an embittered resentful spirit—bitterness—had taken root. I would never lash out with wrath-induced punishment, so I pushed the anger down and it had begun to poison me from the inside. I could not view my supervisor without disdain, and that's not how I should be relating to another human being, especially not when that other human is a sister in Christ. Hebrews 12:14-15 teaches us how to handle situations such as mine.

> Work at living in peace with everyone, and work at living a holy life, for those who are not holy will not see the Lord. Look after each other so that none of you fails to receive the grace of God. Watch out that no poisonous root of bitterness grows up to trouble you, corrupting many (NLT).

I intend to be a woman God can bless. I have to work to live at peace with my supervisor. I have to work at being holy so that I will receive the grace of God. There is only one way to excise a root of bitterness and that is to yank it out by those roots. The tool to work on bitterness weeds that have grown up in our spiritual garden is the tool of forgiveness. Forgiving comes from the Greek word *charizomenoi*, which means "to show favor, to pardon, and to show kindness." Again, although difficult, I need to just release (pardon) my supervisor from my inflamed, bitter clutches. Releasing her releases me. Forgiveness is the antidote for the poison of bitterness.

We can decide to stop holding people accountable to us. Jesus made that decision when dealing with us. He could have exacted the payment from us that we owed. However, He swallowed our sin and nailed it in Himself on the cross. Now He relates to us just as if we'd never sinned (we are justified). Matthew 6:14-15 is clear:

> For if you forgive men their trespasses, your heavenly Father will also forgive you. But if you do not forgive men their trespasses, neither will your Father forgive your trespasses (NKJ).

You may feel as though you could never, ever forgive that cheating spouse who stole the best years of your life, that conniving co-worker who stole your idea and got promoted, that awful thief who shot your son while robbing the store where he worked, or that nasty uncle who robbed you of your innocence. As long as you hold them in bondage to your unforgiveness, you have to serve as the jailer, so you remain with them in the prison of your pain. Let God take your shifts. Leave the unchangeable past behind you and launch into the future that God can bless because "eye has not seen, nor ear heard, nor have entered into the heart of man the things which God has prepared for those who love Him" (1 Corinthians 2:9).

Check Yourself

Facing your true feelings, admitting the anger, and then dealing with it is the work of the tool of forgiveness. Who are you holding in the clutches of your unforgiveness? Admit the anger. It takes energy to continue to clench your teeth, tighten your eyes, and stiffen your posture. Stop expending that energy. Determine to stop letting the person continue to affect your life.

Person I need to forgive/release	What the person did that hurt me and caused my anger	My affirmation of forgiveness
EX: My supervisor	EX: Treated me unfairly by forcing me to stop my action because someone else misunderstood my intention. She did not allow me to face my accuser.	EX: I choose to forgive my supervisor. I will speak with her civilly and work at not allowing this incident to color my future interactions with her. Instead, I will treat future interactions on their own merit.

When someone is angry because she has been accused of doing something she didn't do, I'm sure you've heard people tell her, "Get over it. Let it go. Just forgive and forget!" You will probably never forget the wrong that was done to you; however, if you are committed to snatch the root of bitterness out of your life, you cannot continue to feed yourself on a steady diet of the problem. Life is full. Deliberately put your mind on something else. Also, take care of yourself. Get enough sleep, drink enough water, and read enough of God's Word on a daily basis.

I did these things, and the Lord worked it out so my supervisor and I could talk privately face to face. I admitted how deeply the situation had angered me and how it had started to plant itself as a root of bitterness. I also admitted that the Lord and I had pulled that weed out and I refused to think poorly of her. She confirmed that she didn't have a vendetta against me, and she too was having an anger and bitterness problem over a different situation. We were more alike than different. God has begun to restore our relationship and I'm really glad about that.

R.I.S.E.

Radical change. What is out of whack in my habits, thoughts, or actions that need to be radically changed? What has made you angry to the point of that anger becoming a root of bitterness?

Initiated by God. What is Scripture telling me about being tenderhearted and forgiving?

Submission to the Holy Spirit's direction. How is the Holy Spirit directing me to carry out the tearing out of the root of bitterness that I have found in my heart?

Emergence into full understanding (and readiness to pass the information on). Upon making the necessary

Bitterness versus Being Tenderhearted and Forgiving

lifestyle changes, in what ways am I being led to share my new understanding about bitterness, being tenderhearted , and forgiveness with those around me?

Chapter Thirteen

The Renewed, Bless-able You
Ephesians 4:17–32

So, in conclusion, let's end where we began, with the passage we just studied. In our quest to be women God can bless, we turned to a passage penned by the apostle Paul. Through the inspiration of the Holy Spirit, Paul tells us that we need to stop functioning as if we were people who do not know the Lord. Our understanding has been enlightened because we are no longer alienated from the life of God. We used to have no other choice but to live greedily in our uncleanness.

But now, we have learned that since we are in Christ, we are able to make the right decisions about our conduct. We cannot claim that it's impossible for us to live holy lives. We are fully able to change our ways from how we lived formerly by being renewed in the spirit of our minds. We are fully capable of living as God would want us to live, new women created in true righteousness and holiness.

Since we are able to live right, Paul gives us specific points on which to concentrate.

- Concentrate on telling the truth whenever we open our mouths. Stop lying.
- When we get angry—and we will—remember that we are able to control ourselves, not letting that anger boil over, and not letting Satan, the arch enemy of our souls, gain a foothold to stir up more havoc in our lives and relationships.
- Concentrate on working for what we need and want rather than stealing.
- And pay attention to what we say. Watch our mouths! Do not let any words escape that do not build and bring grace to the hearers.
- Concentrate on making the Holy Spirit smile by replacing bitterness, wrath, anger, clamor, and evil speaking with kindness and forgiveness, in the same spirit of forgiveness we received from God through Christ (Sharon's paraphrase).

We won't be perfect until we get to heaven, but in the meantime, we can do our best to honor God by living as He would have us to live. Lining my thoughts and actions up with this passage is a beginning step. We're not conforming to this standard because we *have to* do so to twist God's arm to bless us. We're conforming to this standard because we *get to* honor God in this way. The good news reality is that God blesses obedience; He's just good like that! Enjoy being a woman God can bless.

Chapter Thirteen

The Renewed, Bless-able You
Ephesians 4:17–32

So, in conclusion, let's end where we began, with the passage we just studied. In our quest to be women God can bless, we turned to a passage penned by the apostle Paul. Through the inspiration of the Holy Spirit, Paul tells us that we need to stop functioning as if we were people who do not know the Lord. Our understanding has been enlightened because we are no longer alienated from the life of God. We used to have no other choice but to live greedily in our uncleanness.

But now, we have learned that since we are in Christ, we are able to make the right decisions about our conduct. We cannot claim that it's impossible for us to live holy lives. We are fully able to change our ways from how we lived formerly by being renewed in the spirit of our minds. We are fully capable of living as God would want us to live, new women created in true righteousness and holiness.

Since we are able to live right, Paul gives us specific points on which to concentrate.

- Concentrate on telling the truth whenever we open our mouths. Stop lying.
- When we get angry—and we will—remember that we are able to control ourselves, not letting that anger boil over, and not letting Satan, the arch enemy of our souls, gain a foothold to stir up more havoc in our lives and relationships.
- Concentrate on working for what we need and want rather than stealing.
- And pay attention to what we say. Watch our mouths! Do not let any words escape that do not build and bring grace to the hearers.
- Concentrate on making the Holy Spirit smile by replacing bitterness, wrath, anger, clamor, and evil speaking with kindness and forgiveness, in the same spirit of forgiveness we received from God through Christ (Sharon's paraphrase).

We won't be perfect until we get to heaven, but in the meantime, we can do our best to honor God by living as He would have us to live. Lining my thoughts and actions up with this passage is a beginning step. We're not conforming to this standard because we *have to* do so to twist God's arm to bless us. We're conforming to this standard because we *get to* honor God in this way. The good news reality is that God blesses obedience; He's just good like that! Enjoy being a woman God can bless.